Cha

Tish

Navigating through the bustling crowds, I tried to hear my sister's voice over the Christmas music playing in the airport.

"Tish, I'm about to go to jail."

"Tasha what do you mean you're about to go to jail? What happened?"

"I accidentally ran a red light, and the cop pulled me over." I heard Noelle crying in the background.

"Why is my baby crying, Tasha?"

"She's just scared of these hoe ass cops. It's okay Aunty baby. Don't cry, we're okay." My irresponsible ass little sister spoke as I stepped onto the escalator.

I'd just landed in Vegas hoping to have a good time with my dearest friends. We haven't had an outing in a long time, and this was our reunion trip. Now Tasha's calling me with this bull shit about getting pulled over. What a hell of a way to start a much-needed vacation.

A girl's trip this close to Christmas sounded crazy at first but it's just the 19th so this three-day visit to Vegas wouldn't stop me from waking up on Christmas Day with my daughter. That's if my sister didn't get her sent to Child Protective Services before then.

"Hold on Tish, he's walking back to the car." She put the phone down just as my friends started calling my name.

"Tish, come on!"

I threw my carry-on bag over my shoulder and did a slight jog to catch up to them.

"Our bags are coming out of the carousel now and the Uber is about to leave us." Krystal rushed, looking like a fool in that big-ass Santa Claus hat. Her Christmas spirit always kicked in immediately after Thanksgiving dinner. I on the other hand wouldn't celebrate holidays if it weren't for my daughter. Lately, I haven't felt like being happy just because it was a holiday. The holiday cheers got sucked right out of me after my mama passed away last Thanksgiving, so I've been fighting to smile simply for Noelle.

I held the phone up to my ear as I grabbed my suitcase and started toward the pickup area. The airport was packed, and people were scrambling to their flights and rides like chickens with their heads cut off. I could tell that Vegas was going to be packed even during the week of Christmas. At first, I thought we would be the only fools coming out here at this time of the year but obviously, this was the place to be.

I haven't gone on a vacation since the Bahamas which was a little over three years ago. I came back from that trip with plenty of souvenirs, most importantly my daughter, Noelle. A one-night stand with the finest man I've ever met left me pregnant by someone I hardly knew. It didn't turn out so bad, but I still didn't really know my child's father to this day. He was just as much of a mystery now, as he was back then. But he took care of our daughter and that's all I could ask for.

My daughter's father, Chill, lives in Chicago while me and my daughter live in Dallas. Since she isn't in school, we do two months with me and two months with him to give us equal amounts of time with her. We rotate holidays and her birthdays, so she will know both of her parents just the same. However, Chill and I were still strangers at best and decided a long time ago that we would co-parent and be nothing more.

"Hey Tish, I'm back."

"What did he say?"

"He said I have a warrant but he's letting me go."

"Thank you, God!"

"Yes, praise him. You see how the Christmas spirit makes people kind and understanding. I love the holidays."

"I highly doubt it's the Christmas spirit that got you out. You probably have those big ass titties peeking out your top as we speak."

"And do." She laughed like something was funny.

"Anyway, get my baby home and y'all need to stay there until I get back."

"For three days, Tish? We still have to eat."

"Doordash then because I don't want you riding around all reckless with my baby."

"So accidentally running a red light is reckless? I was opening a juice for your child when I did."

"Whatever you say. Bye, Tasha." I hung up the phone. I swear my mama left me with a grown-ass child to raise when she passed away. Tasha's always been irresponsible as hell, but back then she was my mama's problem and not mine. Now I was having to loan her money, listen to her whine about working, and check the jail roster every night just to make sure she hadn't gotten locked up. Stuff like that, I never had to think about before but now it was my responsibility. Mama, why did you have to leave me?

Once we found our Uber, we loaded our luggage and climbed inside the backseat. The driver didn't have Christmas music blasting like our ride to the airport which I could appreciate. That lady earlier restarted Jingo Bell Rock five times in a row giving me an early morning headache.

"Tish what was your sister talking about? Everything okay with Tweet?" my friend, Dixon called my baby by her nickname.

"Yes, she's good. My sister is just irresponsible as hell, and I don't know why I left my baby with her."

"Why didn't you just send her with her daddy?"

"Because it's his month off and I didn't want to bother him. This is just a quick turnaround trip anyway. I'll be back in Dallas opening toys with my baby for the holidays."

"Well, I didn't get my kids nothing but clothes. They have so many toys their daddy found a leggo in my ass the other night."

"Noelle too and I wish I had the power to tell her no but she's so cute." I looked at the picture of her on my screensaver. Because I only had one child, holidays were easy to prepare for. Starting in August I bought my baby a toy every week so when Christmas came, I didn't have to stress about getting it all at once. After all, it was hard competing with her father who sent her stuff to our house every day. Noelle had more designer than me and I'm almost 30 years old. My baby daddy obviously had money.

When we got to the MGM hotel, the Uber driver dropped us off in view of the tall lit Christmas tree in the pickup area. When we walked inside there were gift boxes surrounding their signature lion in the lobby. I got an overwhelming scent of coffee and mint from the nearby Starbucks and the Christmas music was serenading everyone in the busy lobby. As much as I hated Christmas songs, I even found myself singing along to a few as we got checked in.

After getting our key we went up to our rooms and changed pretty quickly to make it to this night club we prepaid for. Krystal had set an itinerary and wanted us on time for everything. Her full itineraries and us getting drunk all day was always a recipe for a good time.

Our first stop was a day party inside Drai's Night Club located at the Cromwell Hotel. Dixon and Krystal walked through security first but when it was my turn, he stopped me in my tracks.

"You can't bring this purse in here. No handbags bigger than a wallet." He pointed towards my purse on my shoulder.

"Are you serious?"

"Dead ass."

"You can't just let me slide?"

"No, I cannot. You think because you fine, I'm going to bend the rules for you? I see fine women all day everyday baby. This is Vegas. Get rid of the purse or I can't let you in." He showed no mercy. We stepped to the side of the line and the girls instantly started complaining.

"Just throw the purse away Tish. It sounds like it's already jumping in there and going back to the room is going to take too much time."

"No! I'm not throwing away my only designer purse. This is real Louie and I bought it for myself last Christmas." I snapped.

"Chill?"

"I am chilling Dixon, I'm not yelling."

"No Bitch, Chill, your baby daddy, he's right over there." When I turned, I saw Chill walking up to security I hadn't seen him in person in years so what were the fucking odds to see him in Vegas. He always sent someone else to get Noelle at the airport. I only knew what he looked like because his face was etched in my head for months after our one-night stand.

"Wow, that is him."

"Yeah, I know. Definitely can't mistake him for anybody else." Dixon all but physically drooled over my baby daddy.

Chill was about 6'3 so he truly wasn't hard to spot in a crowd. When I first met him, I genuinely felt like I'd met a God. His strong broad shoulders and his perfect facial structure went hand and hand into making one perfect man. Brown sugar skin, beautiful dark waves, and lips that looked sweeter than frosted sugar cookies. Chill had swag and he always held himself in a calm demeanor. He seemed to be a man of little words and one who had the power to stop the world if he wanted to. Our night together was magical, and I haven't had sex half as good since. My cooch still thought about Chill even when my mind didn't want to.

"Tish, why you just staring at him? We should go say hi."

"Hi for what? He's obviously here doing his own thing and so are we."

"Yeah, but he's chopping it up with the security guards. He can probably get us in with your lil Who-ie Vuitton."

"Ha, Ha funny bitch."

"But for real, you should go say hi. He's a good daddy to Noelle. He would appreciate it." Krystal was always pushing me to be a good person since she was so positive. I exhaled deeply and then walked over to his group stopping him just before he walked into the club.

"Wait, Chill." I grabbed his arm and one of the guards grabbed me like I did something wrong. Chill turned back over his shoulder and said,

"She good, this Noelle mama."

"Oh, my bad boss man." The guard quickly unhanded me.

"Baby mama. What are you doing in Nevada?" He smiled, as he squinted his eyes looking at me from top to bottom. On the bottom row of his teeth, he had a Diamond grill that made his mouth glisten when he talked. His top row was white as snow showing his real teeth looked just as expensive as the diamonds.

"I'm here with my girls. What about you?" I asked, stuttering over my words because he was so fine, he made me nervous. On top of his stature, he smelled like mint mixed with Amber, cocoa powder, and fresh linen. It was the same way he smelled in Jamaica, so this must've been his favorite cologne or natural scent.

"I have a couple businesses out here, so this is my second home. Who got my baby?"

"My sister Tasha."

"Oh, auntie TT. She talks about her all the time."

"Those two are real life besties." I replied, clearing my throat because it got a little quiet.

"Why y'all standing off to the side? You tried to bring weed in here?"

"No, they said my purse is too big. He said I needed to take it back or I couldn't get in."

"No you don't. Y'all come on." Chill replied signaling for Krystal and Dixon to walk towards us. Chill walked us through the security without saying a word or paying for entry. After hitting a side hallway, we were met with a group of niggas who also looked like money. There were too many diamonds, silk shirts, and expensive jewelry to count. Every one of these men were fine but none as handsome as Chill. He was just different and godly in my opinion.

"Damn Chill what took you so long Bruh? We were about to leave your big mysterious ass." I recognized Chill's little brother Nick talking shit. He always called Noelle on her iPad and I got a few glimpses of him from time to time. I also saw him on Instagram where he had almost half a million followers.

Nick was a few inches shorter than Chill and had curly black hair on the top of his head. His edge up was as crisp as I'd ever seen before, and he had those same strong dominant features as Chill. Nick's fashion swag was however different from Chill's. He wore loud colors, and off-the-wall patterns which ironically came together. Like right now he had on red pants and a sweater with a black Santa on the front smoking weed. I couldn't picture Chill wearing something like this, but it worked for him so I'm sure he gets plenty of bitches.

"How y'all going to leave the nigga with the key to the balcony suite. I was talking to Tish." He nodded his head to me.

"Tish? Wait my niece here?" His eyes lit up as he approached me. He hugged me like we were family and held his arm around my waist.

"No, she's at home with my sister."

"Aww man, you should've brought her. I would've stayed at home to keep her. I miss her little pretty self."

"Yeah, me too and it hasn't even been a full day since I left."

"Well, it's nice to meet you, Tish. It's nice to meet all of you. I'm actually going to stay downstairs for a minute." He lowered his glasses to look at some exotic-looking females who passed by.

"It was nice meeting y'all though. Maybe I will see y'all fine asses later."

He walked off showing his playboy ways.

When the elevator opened everyone started to file inside and Dixon was so excited, that she pinched me on my arm.

We rode up to the 4th floor listening to dreams and nightmares over the speaker. When the elevator opened, there was a view of the huge Drais neon sign. We were high up above the dance floor and had the perfect view of Vegas from here.

"Okay this view is lit. Alright baby daddy." Krystal nudged me after pulling out her phone. She started recording everything around us while I simply took it all in. This was just the refresher I needed.

"Bitch were in the presidential section. Your baby daddy must have money money." Krystal said into my ear.

"Yeah, obviously."

"Now girls, let's get a drink from the bar. Start turning on up." Dixon shimmied her shoulders, and we followed behind her. At the personal bar, I got a straight glass of vodka with an ice sphere to cool the burn. Dixon got her favorite drink Incredible Hulk and Krystal got her favorite, Lemon Drop. We went over to the railing to look down over the entire club and enjoy our drinks. Every female knows drinks are even better when they're free. The lights in here were illuminating making this a pulsating oasis. The music was thumping, sparklers were in the air, and it looked more like New Year's Eve than Christmas in here.

As we stood by the rail dancing, a guy in Chill's crew approached us. After him, two more came and then we were surrounded. The first guy had long dreads and a grey beanie on his head with an unbuttoned shirt. His body was nice, his eyes were a chestnut brown, and he stood taller than everyone in here except Chill.

"How are y'all ladies doing? I'm Keys, this is Snoopy, and this is Jack?" He pointed to the other men standing around us. Snoopy was about 5'9 which made him look tiny next to the rest of them. Jack was average height and dark-skinned which was Dixon's type. Only she would diss him for something so small like his shoestrings being too tight.

"We're good." We said in unison like some birds. We've been friends since college, so we all picked up the same habits. Though we acted alike we were all much different. Anybody hanging around us long enough could see that.

"That's what's up, I see y'all sipping out of these glasses. Taking it easy huh." Keys commented, taking a bottle of Hennessy to the head.

"What are we supposed to be drinking out of? Our hands?" Dixon asked.

"Nah, a bottle. You in the club partying with the owner. Take advantage of being around niggas like us while you can."

"Which one of y'all the owner?" Krystal asked.

"My boy Chill over there. He just bought the old owners out. Why you think we way up here? My nigga taking over the Vegas club scene one night club at a time."

I must say I'm impressed because buying a club in Vegas couldn't have been for a small amount of money. Which meant he was more than a millionaire as I originally thought. It was always just a guess because I never knew exactly what he had because I never filed child support on him. He paid our rent up for a year the past two years and deposited ten grand a week into my bank account, even when Noelle was with him. He always told me to let him know if I needed anything but the money he sent was more than enough. I had a saving of over 100,000 from his deposits alone because I never touched it. That was money I was giving Noelle when she turned eighteen. No one else knew I had it like that because people would have their hands out on a regular.

"So y'all live around here? How y'all know Chill?" Snoopy asked just as Chill approached our group. He took a cup of liquor to his mouth and then licked his lips.

"Y'all niggas over here trying to mack already? Let the ladies get settled in first."

"Shid it's hard when they look like this." Jack finally spoke.

"Well look at anybody else in here tonight but this one." He pointed at me. I don't know why I was flattered but I was. What exactly did he mean?

"Oh, so that's how you know him. My bad bruh, I didn't know this was your woman."

"Technically it's not. This is Noelle mama." He clenched his jaws.

"Oh shit, I ain't know."

"Yeah, so none of y'all niggas say shit to her because ain't nobody in here good enough to be a stepdaddy to my daughter. I'll kill one of you niggas straight up." Krystal and Dixon both grinned as they watched the show.

"Damn, none of us? What kind of nigga is good enough?"

"A dead one." He gave him an icy glare. He then walked away, and the attention went away from me like the light from a broken lamp. I don't know if I was mad or flattered about Chill shutting all of them down. However, I can admit, that what he said about a dead stepdaddy was both wild and sexy, especially with the liquor flowing through my system.

Chill went to sit back down on the couch in the back of the section and Krystal and Dixon were still being flirted with by Keys and Snoopy. Jack found another chick in here to give his time, so I was left standing alone getting tipsy. I don't know why Krystal was giving these niggas her time because she was happily married and had been for years. She met her husband Leon at UNT, the school we all graduated from. He was the perfect husband, and they had the perfect family which I kind of envied. If I had what she had I wouldn't look towards another man. After all, she never had to worry about a man like Leon cheating on her.

Drowning myself in liquor, I took Keys earlier advice and got a bottle of rum from behind the bar and took a seat on the tall bar stool by the railing. The ambience here was one of a kind and I'd never seen a more beautiful club. I pulled out my phone to record just in time for a confetti cannon to shoot out over the dance floor. An exhilarating feeling covered my body and I instantly wanted to be a part of it. I slowly climbed down from the barstool and approached the girls.

"Hey, let's go downstairs for a little while. It's lit down there and I want a confetti falling video."

"How do we get down there?"

"I don't know!"

Krystal and I yelled back and forth to one another.

"There's an elevator right there that goes straight downstairs." Keys chimed in pointing towards some elevator doors.

"Let's go bitches, we'll be back sexy." Dixon rubbed her hand across Key's exposed chest. He bit his lip and followed Dixon's ass all the way over to the elevator. I pushed the button to go down the doors slid open exposing the gold-plated walls that were inside.

"Let's take a picture." Krystal pulled out her camera and we stopped dancing only long enough to pose. I may be shy and reserved most of the time but when I was drunk, I was outgoing and the complete opposite. That's why people always invited me out with them to have fun. I even partied with some of my coworkers from the firm I worked for. Being a paralegal was honestly a cool job.

Once we got to the bottom floor and the door slid open, the energy sucked us out like a vacuum.

... I can't be fucked with, no

Hoe you can't touch this, ay.

The DJ had good music playing and the littest part was all the many races all congregated together as one. You didn't see this kind of stuff in Texas. Most clubs were segregated by race by choice.

I don't be stressin' 'bout none of these niggas. When they be talkin', I don't even listen. Tellin' me secrets, I probably forget it, But I'ma tune in when he say he gon' lick it.

"Come on Tish. Shake all of that ass." Krystal started hyping me up. I was tipsy so I bent over to shake my ass because it had been a while. My ass moving like jello of course drew attention from men around us. I felt a man's pelvis start to press up against me and I looked at Dixon to see her facial expression. She raised her eyebrows with a dimpled smile which meant he was cute. If he wasn't she would've snatched me up so quick, and we would've been halfway across the dance floor by now.

Me and the guy danced to the beat until it switched, and I finally turned around to look him in the face. He was a handsome man, looked of Asian descent but not the typical slanted eyes and square faces. He was tall, slender, and had some American features. Maybe he was biracial or some shit.

Because the music down here was so loud, he had to press his lips up against my ear to talk.

"Hello, I'm Jeremy."

"Hey, I'm Tish. Nice to meet you." I stuck my hand out to shake his.

"Same here, where are you from?"

"Dallas."

"What was that?" He pointed at his ear.

"Dallas."

"Oh okay. I'm from Austin. Small enough world right." He kept bouncing to the music.

"Do you ladies want a drink?" We got top-shelf tequila in our section."

"Sure, we will take one."

"We're right over here." He led me off the dance floor. I grabbed Krystal's wrist and she attached to Dixon's to navigate through the crowd. When we got to their section, we were met by three more men in suits and ties whose eyes seemed to light up seeing three pretty black girls enter their section. They jumped up sticking their hands out to shake ours and as we were greeted one by one, Gage started fixing our drinks.

"Not we on Wall Street." Krystal whispered into my ear. I had to laugh because she was always saying something off the wall. Had to love her ass.

"Here you go beautiful ladies." Gage handed us each a cup.

"This is Carl, Brock, and Galvin. We're all here for Galvin's bachelor trip. He's tying the knot with my sister Allison on Christmas day."

"Aw that sounds so sweet. A Christmas wedding. Congratulations." Krystal held her glass in the air. Everyone with a cup connected them in the air to toast before we took a drink. As I lifted my cup to my mouth, an arm came swatting our glasses down so quickly we didn't have time to react. The cold liquor spilled all over my feet and I turned around ready to cut up only calming down when I saw it was Chill glaring at us.

"Chill, why did you do that? You got liquor all over us."

"Tish, go back upstairs."

"Why? We're having fun down here. What's your problem?

"I'll tell you when I get back upstairs but until then you need to go."

"Chill, what's going on?"

His forehead creased and his eyes narrowed.

"Listen, you mean a lot to somebody who means a lot to me and the last thing I want to do is tell her that some shit happened to you on my watch. Now go back to the elevator and go back upstairs. All of y'all and trust I'm not asking."

"Whatever you say Chill."

We all walked out of the section leaving Chill standing there. The security guard near the elevator opened it for us and we boarded it quietly until Krystal broke the silence.

"Tish, I know that's your baby daddy, but can I just say that was the sexiest shit I've heard in a long time. Go back upstairs, all of y'all." She imitated his raspy voice. We all started to giggle like schoolgirls and I had a schoolgirl-type feeling in my stomach. I was crushing on my baby daddy whom I still hardly knew much about. I'm not sure what just set him off, but I got the vibes that he wasn't the one to cross so I was going to listen. Back to the president's box, I go because my baby daddy said so. Never thought I would say those words.

Chapter 2

Chill

When I snapped twice two of the club security guards rushed the section. Grabbing these white boys up by their necks, they quickly moved them into a small room down one of the back hallways. I followed behind them and entered the room taking off my shirt at the door because I didn't want to get blood on it.

Tito and Big Tee gagged their mouths because they knew I didn't like to hear grown men cry. I even tried to instill in my two-year-old daughter that tears were a sign of weakness. It was just a way to express that you are a bitch in my opinion.

"I'll make this quick because I'm not here to work tonight. Inside each section we got a camera, and, on those cameras, I saw y'all putting pills inside a bottle of liquor y'all just tried to pass to my baby mama. Now where I come from, that's a crime punishable by death."

They all started to shake their heads with tears running down their face. I scratched in my beard as I stared them down.

"Now, there's two things I don't play about. That's my businesses, and my family. Tonight, y'all fucked with both of them. It pains me that I have to risk my freedom by murking y'all, but I just can't let this shit go." I took my gun from my waistband.

Muffled screams came from their mouths but that didn't faze me. I've been a murderer since I was seventeen. Killing folks was second nature to me.

POW POW POW POW

I shot all four of them in the head and they dropped like flies. The music in the club drowned out the noise but the room was still filled with the smoky scent of gunpowder.

"Take them to the cremation center in Boulder City. Get Ike to wipe the cameras down after y'all leave."

"On it boss."

I checked the mirror inside the room to make sure there was no blood on me. When everything checked out, I left to go back to the part of the club where I felt most safe. Don't get me wrong, I feared nothing but the jealousy that a man like me attracts. That could for sho get me killed in the world we are in today.

After reaching the suite, I sat on the couch and took a shot of the liquor sitting on the table. The burning sensation oozed down my throat and within seconds, it calmed me down. I bobbed my head to the music only looking up when I spotted thick brown legs standing in front of me. Her legs seemed to go up a mile before they reached her black leather dress.

"Hey, Mr. Chill. I told you I would be here." Monique replied, fluttering her eyelashes as she looked down towards me.

My preference for women were all over the place. If you looked good, I would fuck you with not many more requirements. I've drove black, white, fat, and skinny women up the wall before. Picky men didn't have the passion for pussy like I do. Truth is, I was chasing a high in sex that I've only had a few times in my life.

I stood to my feet now towering over her as she gripped her bottom lip with her teeth. I took my fingertips up her arm gliding them over the goosebumps forming over her skin.

My touch always made women shiver. It was one of the reasons why I went by the name Chill in the first place. That and my always calm demeanor. Even as a kid, I didn't sweat much.

"So, you came back to visit the club after all. I like that."

"You like what?"

"That you listen when a real nigga speaks."

"Listen? You mean take your advice." She moistened her lips.

"Advice goes into your ears and then up to your brain. That entire process is called listening. Just like if I put my dick deep inside your pussy, that's process is called fucking. You will also listen that way too."

"You're so damn cocky, but you're right. Everything you say is so right." She rolled her eyes with a lustful grin on her face.

I'd only met Monique a few weeks ago at the airport in the American Express lounge. She was here for a photo shoot, and I was at the airport to fly out to Atlanta to purchase some property. She told me she only dated millionaires and I let her know I fit that description times a thousand. I was on Billionaire status after years of grinding and making the right moves. There were only 5% of billionaires that were black and I'm probably the only real nigga in that percentile.

Monique and I sat down on the couch and my baby mama Tish approached me.

"Where is the restroom since I can't communicate with no men in here?" She still had an attitude from me getting on her ass earlier, but I ain't give a fuck. I was watching her ass like a hawk until she left Vegas. I would die trying to protect Noelle's heart because I know her mama is her world.

"There's one over there behind the bar." I pointed and she stormed off. You could see the curiosity on Monique's face, but she knew not to question me. I didn't answer to anybody but the man living inside my head. Or shit the men in there when I'm really on demon time.

The neon signs, LED screens, and strobe lights made vibrant colors dance all over the club. In the club industry, the lighting was more important than the DJ or what's behind the bar. Lights made bitches feel sexy, they electrified your soul and gave you a natural ecstasy that darkness couldn't do. I knew when I went into the club industry that I would take over just as I did in every other avenue in my life.

"Your eyes are almost glowing in here. I don't think I've ever saw eyes so brown." Monique was nestled under me looking up into my face as I sipped from my glass.

"Thanks. Are you having fun out here or you want me to show you my little office in the back?"

"What's in there?"

"An orgasm or two or shit three depending on how much you can take." I licked my lips as I rubbed up her exposed thigh.

"You're so sexy."

"So that means I can fuck you, right?"

"Of course, just lead the way." She stood from the couch, and we walked into the back left corner where my little office sat.

"Take all your clothes off. Your shoes too."

"Why do I need to get completely naked?"

"Because I'm about to touch every part of your body. Hurry up." I growled into her ear. She did as I said removing her clothes from her frame seductively. I waited patiently until she was bare from head to toe and then I began devouring her breast like two pieces of fruit. Sucking her titties, I traced each nipple with my tongue before gripping them gently with my teeth. I picked her up from the ground and in one motion, I pushed my dick deep inside of her.

"Fuck, so much dick. So much dick." She cried out before biting on my neck. I fucked her hard touching her guts every time gravity slid her back down. After fucking her like that for a while, I dropped her feet to the floor and turned her around smacking her ass a few times because of the hump in her back.

"Nah baby, get right. Let me see that arch." Her back caved in just how I needed it to.

I slid inside her inch by inch until I couldn't see my dick anymore. I entered her guts for only a few strokes before she started running away from me. Grabbing her by her shoulder I tried keeping her in place, but she just couldn't take all this dick at once. I knew everything about a woman's body, and mine was made to please so I backed out a little and gave her just the amount of dick she wanted.

"Fuck Chill, I'm about to cum. I'm about to cum!"

She started to shake and cream, leaving a trace of her pleasure down my dick. I didn't nut because she didn't let me fuck her how I needed to. There's only one bitch I ever dealt with in my life took that dick just how I wanted, and that was Tish. She was dangerous to me because of that and that's the reason I never doubled back. I would have six kids by now fucking with a bitch like her.

After I pulled out of her pussy, I made her drop to her knees to clean it off with her mouth.

"You so blessed baby, but that's something I could tell from a far." She licked my dick like a melting ice cream cone. When she was done, she stood up thinking we were about to kiss, and I backed away.

"Are we going back out there or we going to your place for round two?"

"I'm about to roll out. You can stay at the club if you want."

"What does that mean? Don't you want to hang out?"

"We just did."

"Chill what do you mean we just did? I came out here to see you and I booked a flight home for after Christmas. I planned on being with you until then."

"Christmas? I'm not even spending Christmas with my daughter so I'm damn sure not spending it with you. Enjoy Vegas." I grabbed the door handle and stepped out of the room. She left behind me and went straight to the elevator. She was mad and so was I. I just wasted my time with yet another bitch who can't take dick.

Chapter 3

Dixon

"Fuck yes, right there."

I moaned as Keys and I stood up in the corner. It was dark over here so I'm sure everyone thought we were just kissing but he was taking his finger in and out of my pussy like a maniac. In my opinion, the only way to fuck a pussy is to pound it so this shit felt amazing. Satisfying me sexually was important. It was almost as important as what a man has in his bank account.

The feeling of his three fingers at the right speed made me have a powerful orgasm. Within seconds I was drenching his hand with my warm nectar trembling like a tambourine. It helped that Keys was fine as hell, with caramel skin, long dreads, and sexy tattoos all over his neck. He looked like he was a hoe but fuck it, for a fine ass nigga I was too.

I was 28 years old, working as a nurse at the hospital but I didn't necessarily like people. The check, along with pressure from my mama is what made me end up in nursing school.

I was a pretty girl, with long thick hair, beautiful brown skin, a flat tummy with a dimpled back. I was way too pretty to be cleaning up mucus and blood that came out of different people. I couldn't wait until my big break when the right nigga came along, and I could hang up my scrubs once and for all.

"It looks like my homies about to roll. Y'all coming with us?"

Keys asked as he pulled his hand from my panties.

"Coming where? Back to your hotel room?"

"Nah, the penthouse. Chill just brought one at the Pslams resort which is a couple miles away from here."

"I'm down if my girls are."

"Good. I'm not done with your lil' ass yet." He walked over to Chill.

Krystal was sitting on a nearby couch in between Jack and Snoopy. She was just running her mouth with them because her lanky ass was faithful to her husband, too faithful if you asked me. I spotted Tish who was sitting by herself looking out over the dance floor as she drank out of a bottle.

"Bestfriend, you okay?"

"Yeah, girl I'm good. Drunk so I'm great actually. You calling us an Uber?" She got so close to my face that I could smell the rum seeping from her pores.

"We got invited over Chill's house to vibe some more. You down?"

"No girl, I'm good. I need to go to the room and lay down until the world stops spinning so fast." She fell off the barstool and I had to catch her.

"Are you sure? Here, let me help you."

We walked towards the elevator door where everyone was walking into.

"Yes, I'm sure, y'all have fun."

"Okay. Krystal, you going back to the room with Tish?"

"No, I'm still having a blast. Why is she going to the room?" Krystal asked, slightly tipsy but still not as fucked up as Tish.

Before everyone got into the elevator Chill spotted us holding her up.

When he walked over to us, I looked up into his eyes and instantly got nervous. He was so intimidating in the sexiest way possible.

"Y'all got a ride from here?"

"We're going to your place; Keys invited us there. Tish is going to the hotel though."

"The hotel with who?" He raised an eyebrow.

"In an Uber I guess, or we drop her off, she definitely can't walk."

"No shit."

Chill was so fine his attitude was something I'm sure got looked over by plenty of women. Someone with so much money and power could honestly talk to me in any kind of way he wants. He was the type of nigga to get his plate fixed and his water ran in the tub every night. Fine, tall, stubborn, and handsome. If Tish hadn't had him first, then I would definitely be on him. But trust, one of his homeboys would do.

"She not going anywhere by herself this drunk. She coming with us. Aye." He got him boys' attention.

"Y'all help them get my baby mama to the car."

The way Chill's large C necklace was shining in the dark illuminated him wherever he went. Glistening like glitter I could tell it was worth millions.

We rode the elevator down to the first floor and came out to a bunch of commotion. People were all around staring as Chill's brother started a shoving match with some dudes. I forgot his ass was here since he dipped away hours ago.

Chill and the rest of the boys ran over to his little brother who dropped a dude to the ground with one punch. They grabbed him up and forced him out of the hotel to the pickup area where three SUVs were lined up.

"Man let me go knock the nigga out one more time," Nick demanded while talking to Chill.

"Bruh get your ass in this car. You fighting in a million dollars' worth of jewelry. Fuck wrong with you?"

"I don't tolerate disrespect. That's what's wrong with me." He got in Chill's face.

"You tolerate whatever until you come get me," Chill growled at his little brother. They sounded like me and my older sister any time we went anywhere. I was the rowdy one who would fight the way to the restroom and one on the way back. I calmed down a lot when I met Krystal and Tish. They showed me that being the bigger person was necessary in some situations. That was that two-parent home logic they were brought up in.

Once everyone was loaded into the cars, the driver started blasting a Lil' Baby song I never heard before. It was a three-seater SUV so we girls were in the back and Scooby and Keys were in the middle section. Chill and his brother rode in a separate car since they were still arguing about the fight he had.

The lights from the strip streamed past the windows and every so often we passed by a Christmas tree, or a fake Santa strolling down the street. Even with Santa being drunk I was still getting the feels for the holidays. With my mama being in prison those feelings were sometimes hard to come by. Her bad checks and bad decisions were going to affect my life drastically for the next six years.

Keys started fumbling around in his pocket taking my attention away from the scenery. He pulled out a thick white tube and then inside was the biggest blunt I had ever seen.

"Y'all ready to get high as the North Pole?" He asked, sticking the blunt in his mouth.

"None of us smoke." Krystal spoke up.

"That's weak as hell but shit more for me." He lit up the blunt. Watching him exhale the smoke from his nostrils was sexy as hell to me. I always had a thing for bad boys and men who lived life on the edge.

My phone chimed from my lap, and I looked over to Tish who was leaning on my shoulder. When I realized she was asleep I unlocked my phone and went to my messages.

"I know you're out with my daughter, but when you have time, please call me. I miss you; I love you." I read the message from Tish's father Winston. Our friendship into a situationship was quite complicated and I couldn't explain how it evolved. It went from me being there for him when Mrs. Eve died to him kissing me one night near the fireplace on the 4th of July. It was kind of weird because I liked him a lot but thinking of Tish's reaction made me never want to get too serious. Plus, I was scared he wouldn't satisfy me in bed and that would mess up the spark I had with him. Plenty of sparks have been put out because of that.

"Oh my God." Krystal griped before leaning over towards my ear to whisper.

"Girl, Leon keeps asking me to let him know when I get back to the room so he can FaceTime me."

"Why is he even up? Ain't it like close to midnight there."

"He's not in Texas remember. He's on the road taking a load to California."

"Just tell him you about to go to sleep and we're asleep too. He will be alright."

"Yeah, he has no other choice."

Krystal started typing on her phone. Seconds later she gasped loudly.

"Read this." She held her hand over her mouth, and she put her screen in my face.

Sorry, we just got to the room and we all going to sleep. I'll talk to you in the morning.

Underneath was a message from Leon with a picture of our room number at the hotel with the caption.

So, are we lying to each other now? I'm here at your room door. Don't forget you put this room on my card. I gasped as loud as she did which made Keys and Snoopy turn around in their seats.

"Yo, y'all alright?" They asked both coughing from the smoke.

"Actually, we are not, I need to go back to our hotel now." Krystal announced making them both smack their lips.

"Man, we're almost to Chill's spot."

"I know, I'm sorry but it's an emergency."

"Krys you sure we need to go back now? You already gotten caught."

"Dixon this is my marriage on the line. I have to go back. It's not an option." She snaked her neck as she spoke. They told the driver to take her back to the MGM Grand but I was staying with them and keeping Tish with me so I wouldn't be alone. What Krystal has going on is why settling down sometimes sounded scary to me. Popping up on a girl's trip was only some shit a married nigga would do.

I'll pass on that matrimony shit.

Chapter 4

Krystal

The driver let me out in the pickup area which wasn't as busy as earlier. The cold desert air whipped across my body, and I wrapped my arms around my waist. I spotted Leon across the driveway sitting on the bench with his head towards the ground. He was wearing a light windbreaker jacket and some jeans, so I knew he was still freezing. Leon has always been handsome, and his bedroom eyes got me at first glance. He had thick hair on his head and his eyebrows grew like hairy caterpillars. He was still the most handsome man in the world to me and I never wanted anyone else. From crushing on him to saying I do, he was always the man for me.

"Babe, you want to go sit inside?" I stuck my hand out to help him, only for him to move it from his face.

"I'm good out here. I need to be cool because the fire I feel inside of me could hurt someone right now."

"Baby, I had no idea you were coming. You told me you had to drive to California when you left earlier this week."

"And I did, I drove straight there only getting about five hours of sleep the entire trip to make it to you. I parked at a trucker's lot, got a rental car, and drove up here to spend the next day and a half with you since I never spent a Holiday away from you until now. I regret it though, obviously you came here to do your own thing."

"That's not true at all. We were at the club and Tish's baby daddy offered for us to come eat at his penthouse. I admit I wasn't honest but that's because I didn't want you to get mad."

He sucked his teeth and shrugged his shoulders as he mumbled, "Yeah right."

I could tell he didn't believe a word I said, and he was angry rightfully so. Leon and I had been together since college. He was the perfect daddy, perfect husband, perfect lover. People often doted on the fact that my life was picture-perfect. This meant that we put on great for the public because our lives weren't all together. Truth is, Leon was let go from his last trucking company and was having trouble finding a new steady job. All he could do was pick up freelance jobs when they popped up and use his granddaddy's rig when he wasn't. That's why he was working through the holidays because Grandpa was off for the winter which allowed Leon to work all month long. I had a check coming in monthly from the school district but being a teacher paid the same as asking what sauce you want with your nuggets. The only reason I could afford this trip was because Leon sold his motorcycle and gave me $500 as a late birthday gift.

"Babe, can we please just step inside."

"I told you I'm out here cooling off. Go to your room." He shooed me with his hand. The wrinkles set into his forehead made his face look unapproachable. I hadn't seen my husband this mad since he first lost his job driving for Pepsi.

"Where are you staying tonight? Am I going with you?"

"I booked a room here at this expensive ass place. Waste of money."

"It's not a waste Leon. We can still go inside."

"No, we can't. I don't know where you been or what you been doing, I don't want to be around you." He gave me a grimacing stare.

"Leon don't act like this. I didn't do anything."

"Krystal please go lie to somebody else!" He said loudly, grabbing the attention of the few people stumbling through the hotel doors. After realizing we were causing a scene he got up and started across the driveway into the hotel.

"Leon, baby!"

I called his name from behind several times, but he didn't answer. I knew he was mad when he went through the door and didn't hold it for me. He was walking so fast it was obvious he didn't want me following him.

Just let him cool off and he will be fine. I told myself, trying not to cry. I was standing in the lobby near the first pair of machines trying to hold my emotions in. I was still in these high heels, so my feet were desperately telling me to have a seat. I sat down at the first machine I saw which was a big Wheel of Fortune game. The brightness from the screen almost blinded my eyes as I held my head up by my fist. I closed my eyes praying for Leon to forgive me until a man's voice started to speak over my thoughts.

"Why you look so sad? My brother and them kicked y'all to the curve." I opened my eyes and saw it was Chill's brother Nick sitting there clicking on the machine.

"Oh, hi, and of course not. I asked to come back here on our way over there. What are you doing here?"

"My brother mad at me for fighting at his club, so I didn't want to go to his crib just yet. I always hit on these machines, so I came here." Nick was way calmer than he was just earlier at the club. He was a cutie for sure with his smooth almond-colored skin and soft pink lips. Above his lip was a small mole or a beauty mark as my grandma would say. The resemblance between him and his brother was almost uncanny. They had the same facial features; the only difference was their skin tones and builds.

"Our of all the hotels in Vegas this is the one you've won at the most. Should I be playing this machine instead of using it as a pillow."

"Hell yeah. I've won twenty-five thousand dollars off a $100 bet on these machines. Here, have a try. Yo first spin is on me." He said, slipping me a piece of paper that read voucher, and $244 on it.

"Are you giving this all to me?"

"Yeah. It's yours. I got plenty more in my pocket." He maintained eye contact and the most captivating smile covered his face. I slipped the voucher into the machine, and it instantly started to roar with lights, bells, and sound effects as if I'd won already.

I didn't know what I was doing so I started pushing max bet and watching the figures scroll across the machine.

When a waitress in elf ears walked by Nick waved her down.

"Ayy, can you give me another Hennessy and coke. Get her one too."

"No, no, I'm done drinking for the night."

"Not until you have a drink with me, two of them." He directed and I laughed and shook my head. To be honest, I probably needed it to numb the pain after me and Leon's big blowout.

"What's your name again?"

"It's Krystal. You're Nick, right?"

"Yeah, how you know that?"

"I remembered when Chill called your name earlier. I'm a teacher. We have no other choice but to learn names quickly."

"Oh true. I should've known you were a teacher. You look smart."

"Look smart, what does that mean?"

"It's a good thing. Better than me saying you look like a dummy."

"That's true." I smirked, as we both continued tapping on our machines.

"What grade you teach?"

"3rd grade. They are the perfect age. They think innocently like babies but are growing into independence like older kids."

"A child's innocence is a special thing. I love my niece past death. I wish I could see her more."

"You're talking about Tweet, right?"

"Yeah, well I call her Noe-Noe. It's a play on her name and the fact that she tells me no any time I try and put her down."

"She is a spoiled baby for sure but she's so sweet. My kids love when she comes over to play."

The waitress came up and sat our drinks in the small area in front of our machines. Nick gave her a $20 bill and she stuffed it inside her fanny pack before walking away.

"Do you have any kids?"

"No, and I don't want any. I like being an uncle but that's as far as it's going."

"I hear that." I started to chuckle as I sipped my drink. I pushed the max bet button a few more times and suddenly my machine became the loudest one in here. The bells started chiming, fireworks started to shoot on the screen, and the jackpot sign started to flash.

Nick's eyes enlarged as he and I looked at my screen.

"Dayum, you hit the jackpot." He smiled in excitement as he got up from his seat.

"Huh, I did? I'm confused."

"What you confused about, you hit that number right there." He pointed at the screen which read $16,235.

"No way, no fuckin way!" I stood up from my seat and started jumping up and down.

"I told you. What I tell you." Nick celebrated with me.

"Oh, my goodness, $16,000, oh my God. Oh my God." I sat back down in my chair and all the attention in the room was on me. Turning to Nick I looked up at him and remembered that it was his money that won this, not mine.

"As long as I can walk away from here with a $1000, I'm cool. It's your money so you should turn this in." I hit the cash-out button and then handed him the voucher slip.

"Nah, nah. This is your money. You won that. I'm happy for you."

"Are you sure? I mean I feel like I owe you this."

"Listen, enjoy your Christmas blessing. I'm good, trust me." He touched me on my shoulder.

"But I have to give you some of it. I want to return the blessing in some type of way."

"Okay then buy me something to eat. There's a food court that way which is open twenty-four hours a day." He pointed across the lobby.

"Well okay, let's go. Where do I turn this in?" I held up the voucher.

"You go to the cashiers because the ATM machines won't dispense that kind of money. Come on, I'll walk you that way." He took his cup up to his mouth and swallowed the liquor leaving nothing but ice. I did the same thing because I now had a spurt of energy I didn't have before.

I couldn't believe I just won, and I could now give my kids and my husband the Christmas they deserve. That's if my husband ever comes around to forgive me.

Nick and I turned in my voucher and I chose the option of receiving a check. I placed it in my purse in my wallet to make sure it was safe and made plans to put it in the bank in the morning.

"Now, for that burger you owe me."

"Let's go." I allowed him to lead our way through the lobby. My head was on a constant swivel hoping to not be seen by Leon. I made sure to walk behind Nick a few steps to be able to play it off if we did run into him. I was prepared to act like I didn't know Nick at all.

He led us to the steak and shake in the food court and he and I both got burgers. He also splurged and got a chocolate shake, and I got their seasonal peppermint mocha shake.

After our order numbers were called, we found a seat and dug into our food. My nerves were on ten because I was praying Leon didn't pop up here. But knowing him, he was in the room for tonight and trying to sleep off his anger.

"You nervous having that check or something?" He snapped me out of my head. My high anxiety must've been showing on my face since I had a hard time hiding it.

"Yes, it's a little nerve wrecking."

"Well don't worry yourself especially as long as you with me. I'm not going to let shit happen to you. So, enjoy your meal."

I did as he said and took a generous helping of my burger into my mouth. I closed my eyes because I hadn't eaten in a while and this was hitting the spot. Since me and him were hungry the table was pretty quiet as we ate. The jolly blend of beats and melodies from Holly Jolly Christmas roared from the steak and shake and I bobbed my head. My homeroom class back home had performed this at the Christmas program just last week. Their tiny voices and Mrs. Frankly on the piano put me in the Christmas spirit even more. I loved spreading the holiday cheer because it was given to me as a kid. Some kids are however receiving the opposite around this time of year. The holiday blues if you will.

"You really like this corny ass music?"

"I love it, you don't?"

"Nah, I listen to niggas like Rod Wave. I don't want to have a Holly jolly shit."

"See that's the problem, you need to switch it up. I wish you could've saw my students sing this song at our Christmas program. They would've brought you some cheer."

"Yeah maybe, but I'm sure I would never have access to something like that. I don't have any kids."

"Well, what about visiting the Las Vegas Sphere. I read somewhere that it will be lit up like a large snow globe starting tonight."

"Yeah, that joint is wild. It's crazy how far technology has come. So what, you trying to go see it?"

"See it when?"

"Shit, right now. We can Uber over there and check it out. That's if you not sleepy."

"I'm not, shoot I honestly would do anything to give you holiday cheer. You deserve to feel that magical feeling on the inside just as I do."

"Oh, you not just feeling Christmas magic right now. You feeling that gambling rush too."

"Shut up."

I hit him on his hand because his cute ass was making me blush.

We threw our trash away and called for a ride. As we walked through the tunnel to the pickup spot, I felt sorta proud walking next to him. I guess it was the jewelry and the way he was walking like he knew he was the hardest nigga in the building. I loved the confidence he exerted and that alone made him even more handsome than he already was.

When we got to the pickup spot, he walked us to an Uber black. The man got out of the car and opened the doors to let us in.

Once in the car, he took us towards the sphere. I enjoyed the view of the dazzling lights that lit up the desert sky. Dallas had a nice skyline, but it wasn't as intertwined as this one. Here every building's light combined and painted one large picture.

My eyes lit up as we approached the dome that displayed the craziest illusion ever. If you didn't know any better, you would think it was a real snow globe in front of us. It was huge and it took me back to my childhood shaking the snow globes on my grandma's tables. I bought a few for my own house last year but the kids broke them acting out PJ Mask in my living room.

"You want to just ride by or get out and take pictures?"

"Mmm, it's cold but this view is too good to pass up. Sir is it okay if we step out for a minute." I asked the Hispanic driver.

"Yeah I guess. You technically get five minutes before I have to leave you."

"Okay, bet. I'll leave you a good tip." Nick replied, opening the car door. We got out and the crisp breeze pierced my skin, but I was sucking it up for the photo.

"Here, I can take a picture of you if you want me to." He took my phone from my hand. Smiling as I smiled, he let me take as many pictures as I wanted. I'm not used to this because Leon would've gotten angry after picture number three. My husband didn't like taking photos and he always felt social media was a waste of time. To him, privacy was more valuable than stunting if you will.

Once I got all the pictures I wanted, we left and directed the driver to return to the MGM. We got only halfway there when Nick leaned up in the seat.

"Hey bruh, can you stop by this lil' corner store right here?" Nick asked the driver who swiftly pulled into the driveway.

"Fuck, my phone just died. I'm just going in here to get a few cigars, you need anything?" He asked me.

"No, I'm okay."

"Bet. One second." He got out of the car and jogged into the store. I mindlessly scrolled through my phone to Leon's page to see if he'd posted anything but of course, he hadn't.

"Does he know those guys? What's going on in there?" The driver said.

I looked up and through the windshield and spotted Nick getting physical with a man after leaving out of the store. Nick was getting the better of him, and the man stepped back pulling a gun from his back pocket.

Pop!

Fired from his gun once and then he ran off.

"Oh my God, he just shot him!"

I got out of the car and ran over to Nick who was lying on the ground bleeding from his thigh.

"We need to put pressure on it. Someone call 911!" I yelled taking my purse off my shoulders and my shirt off in the cold air. When I put my crop top up against his leg he hissed in pain.

"Ahhh, that was them fuck ass niggas I fought at the club tonight. If I die, make sure my brother know that!"

You could see the panic in his eyes, and I was trying to be comforting to him.

"Okay, I will tell him. Just lay back and don't move. The ambulance will be here soon. You will be fine."

I rubbed the side of his face. God knows this boy didn't deserve to die tonight. Especially not because of stupid shit that happened at the club this close to Christmas.

Chapter 5

Tish

When I opened my eyes, I saw floor-to-ceiling windows all around me and I was laid on black suede furniture. A large black 20-foot Christmas tree sat in the corner decorated in all-black ornaments. My purse was on the table in front of me and I hurried to grab my phone to call the girls.

Before I could dial Krystal's number, I heard the sound of a door closing and I was scared to move. Chill's large frame soon emerged from the dark hallway, and I raked my fingers through my hair hoping to not look crazy since I was just knocked out.

"You finally awake, I was coming to make sure you hadn't thrown up on my carpet."

"What time is it?"

"5:00 am." He shocked me with how late it was. Chill was wearing black sweatpants with a black V-neck shirt and what looked to be black Louie slides. He was dressed better than most at this time of the night which attests to him being the flyest nigga I know. I knew he had style because he always sent our baby home with the cutest clothes.

"Do you know where my friends are?"

"One of them is in the spare bedroom with Keys and the other one didn't come."

"Oh okay, I must've blacked out. I don't even remember coming over here." I sat up tugging the bottom of my dress.

"Yeah, I tried waking you up to tell you to get in your daughter's bed, but you didn't budge."

"Noelle has a room here? I thought she had a room at your house in Chicago?"

"She does, but Noelle has a room at all of my houses."

"Dang, that's awesome."

"Yeah, the same lady decorates them all nice and makes them magical for her. You want to see the one here? She picked pink for the walls this time. She changes her favorite color every time I see her.

"Sure, lead the way." I lit up like a kid even with my head pounding. Chill led me through the hallway and as we stepped, motion lights illuminated our path. It was such a luxurious atmosphere because of the high ceilings and beautiful portraits on the walls. When I came to a painting of Noelle that was twice my size I stopped in my tracks.

"Oh my God, this is beautiful. Who did this?"

"An artist named Christen Austin. She's done a few pieces of Noelle for me."

"Wow, she's amazing."

"Yeah, you want one?"

"I would love one but not this big. This size would cover up my entire living room wall."

"Well, do you want me to buy you a bigger living room?" I started to laugh because he had to be joking.

"Yeah right."

"I'm serious. I want y'all to be comfortable. I told you anything y'all need just ask."

"I'll keep that in mind the next time I see a house I like."

"Do that, and it's purchased." He replied, with the most serious look on his face. I broke eye contact with him because looking at him was way too intense. It was like he was touching me with his eyes and every time he licked his lips it was as if his tongue was gliding across mine.

I trailed my fingertips along the painting and then we continued down the hallway.

We eventually stopped at the door with the large glittery pink crown above it. He opened the door, and it was like we'd walked into a castle more specifically the princess's quarters. The room was covered in different shades of pink making such a beautiful monochromatic color scheme. There was a pink train track surrounding the room with a large gold and pink train set making its rounds. Her bed was a canopy and twice the size of my bed at home. There were dressers and shelves on the walls that held small figurines and pictures of her. The room was perfect and the Christmas tree near the lone window in her room made her space even more magical.

"Wow, this is unbelievable. All of this for my baby?"

"Yeah, I mean, she's my baby too."

"I know that I just never thought a kid of mine would have a room like this. You're such a great dad Chill."

"I feel the same way about you. I feel like I got the perfect baby mama."

"Really?"

"Hell yeah. Every time she comes to visit me, she's more and more intelligent. I can tell you put a lot of time and energy into her."

"And like wise. Let me tell you something, she loves her daddy. She's always talking about you and saying she can't wait to see you." He smiled.

"Honestly Chill, don't get me wrong, this is all amazing but I'm just happy to share her with someone I can trust. When I reached out to you on Facebook after I found out I was pregnant I was scared because I felt things could've gone completely differently." He shifted from side to side now avoiding direct eye contact.

"I'm happy you feel that way and you just don't know how much you reaching out to me that day saved my life." He bit his lip nervously.

"You see, I didn't want to be here anymore at the time. My businesses were doing well, I wasn't in any trouble, but I just felt empty. Some days I woke up questioning if I even wanted to live anymore."

"Really?"

"Yeah, that trip I met you on was me attempting to get out of that funk and start to enjoy life again and find meaning."

"Wow, I wouldn't have known you felt like that. You displayed so much confidence when I met you. I remember it radiated from your skin."

"And I was confident. Confident in everything except what my purpose was here. To me, I had reached the ceiling, so what was left for me to do but go backwards. But getting Noelle helped me build a new ceiling to reach. I wanted to be the best father I could be."

"Well, I'm happy that she is blessing your life just as much as she's blessing mine."

"Every damn day."

A female's voice moaned in the distance.

"Did you just hear that?" He looked back over his shoulder.

"Hear what?"

"That bitch moaning loud as hell."

Dixon, I thought to myself. Some would say my friend was easy like Sunday morning. I however felt that she was just sexually liberated. She was single so why not do what she wanted as long as she protected herself?

"At least our friends hit it off right."

"Right." He rubbed the top of his head.

"Can I get you something to drink? Some food?"

"Food, absolutely not but I will take a water if you have some."

"Of course, this way." He led me into the kitchen.

If I didn't think the rest of this house was immaculate, the kitchen would've sealed the deal. The sleek countertops shined from the pendant lights above. The large spacious countertops and the huge center island were filled with small reindeer and Santa figurines. The imitation snow set such a festive scene that I was stuck at the moment with a bright smile on my face.

"You like all this shit? I think it's too much. The interior designer sometimes forgets it's a man that lives here."

He leaned over the center island.

"She is amazing, everything looks so good. I mean I would've never thought to do an all-black Christmas tree, but it works."

"Yeah, it is kinda fly. The water is in that fridge behind you by the way. Pull that long silver handle." He instructed because it was disguised as a cabinet to go with the aesthetic. Inside, everything was so clean and organized as if it had never been touched. I grabbed a bottle of water and then took the longest drink of my life. Chill started chuckling making me a little embarrassed.

"I see where Noelle gets being extra thirsty from. She downs water like a camel in the mornings."

"Hold on, she drinks water here?"

"That's all we drink. What you giving her, sweet ass root beer or something?"

"No Chill. We have apple juice, orange juice, sprite."

"Sugar, Sugar, and more sugar. No wonder my baby be dehydrated."

"Whatever, Chill." I laughed.

"I'm just fucking with you. She's healthy so that's all that matters."

"Right."

"But how are you? Everything good on your end?"

"Yes, everything is good. I'm making it."

"Well, you look good. I see Noelle didn't affect your body at all since the last time I saw you." He turned his lips down as he checked me out.

"Thanks. I work out from time to time."

"Do you? Me too. Maybe we can work out together one day. Push each other to the limit." He flashed a coy smile. Was he flirting with me now?

"That sounds nice but when would we get a chance to do it though?"

"Whenever, I'm always free."

"I highly doubt you're always free. You own one of the most successful clubs in Vegas now. I'm sure other things."

He started to grin.

"Key word, own. I don't have to call in mama. I don't abide by schedules, I set them."

"That's goals. Your whole life is goals actually."

We made eye contact for a lot longer this time with no words. He didn't break his stare only he did a conceited chuckle because he could probably tell I was nervous.

"Damn, yo ass look just like Noelle."

"And she looks just like you when she smiles. You couldn't deny her if you wanted too."

"Of course, I couldn't. Shit, I shut down that speculation a long time ago."

"What do you mean?" I giggled, in a flirtatious manner.

"It means I debunked any of my doubts about her being mine. I got a DNA test done the first time I got her in Chicago." My eyes started to blink rapidly because I was taken aback.

"How, I didn't approve of anything."

"I didn't need you too. I did it through a private company."

"You never told me about this. Why would you do that behind my back?" I squinted my eyes.

"There was no need to tell you. You would've only heard something if it came back negative."

"Oh wow, but it would've been good to know you had doubts about my child." My arms crossed because I was honestly offended. I'm not the type of hoe who wouldn't know who my child's father is. When I had sex with Chill, I hadn't had sex in years. At that time, I was practicing abstinence until his fine ass walked up to me at the bar.

"I mean why wouldn't I have doubts? I barely knew you, Tish."

"You're right. I just wish you told me you were doing that."

"Why?"

"Because I wouldn't have sent my baby off alone with someone who has doubts about her. Period."

"And I wouldn't have given my love to a child I had doubts about, period. Wait, don't tell me you mad."

"I'm not mad, I'm just shocked is all. It's cool I guess."

"No, it's obviously not and I didn't mean to offend you but understand where I'm coming from."

"I'm trying, I will." I corrected my words. Chill walked around the island and stood next to me placing his hand on the small of my back.

"Good, me and you can't have problems or disagreements. It's been peaceful these past few years so let's keep it that way."

"Yeah, but that's probably because we never see each other or talk for that matter."

"Well, we are seeing each other right now so why not make the best of it? I don't want to see you frowning around me so uncross your arms and turn them lips the other way." He lifted my chin and I flashed a smile.

"Now, this is the female who I just had to have that night. You too pretty to ever have a frown across your face."

"And you're too handsome for one, but to be honest I actually kind of like your mug. It's sexy in a way." I couldn't help but simp over him because he was so close.

"Oh, you still attracted to me?"

"Of course, I am. I still think about you and that night often."

"Well, I hope you know I have no problem recreating it?"

"Yeah, and me either." I stared into his eyes. The chills running down my spine made my body tremble and I was so lost in his ora that all I could see was him right now.

"I'll be in my room if you really ready for me. No pressure to come get some pressure love." His voice caressed my ears with a hypnotizing allure. The peppermint scent from his breath traveled up to my nose and the crisp fresh scent of his clothes left an invisible hold on me.

Chill disappeared around the corner, and I followed the magnetic pull he now had on my body. When I stepped inside the room Chill started taking off his shirt and threw it to the ground. He signaled for me to come closer to him and then turned me around to place sensual kisses on my neck.

His hands roamed across my body, and he caressed my breast before reaching down to lift my dress. His hands glided into my panties and his fingers rubbed in between my pussy lips making a subtle moan leave my mouth. Rubbing up and down my clit, he made a sea of juices flow from my pussy as my eyes rolled into the back of my head.

"Does that pussy still taste good?"

"Mmhmm." I tried my best not to cum so fast. Here I was thinking my rose toy made me orgasm quickly, but Chill's fingertips were giving that little machine a run for its money.

"I'm going to taste you real quick so put your hands inside you and touch it just as I was." He guided my hand inside my panties.

"Slow down and do it just like I was." He took his fingers into his mouth and smacked his tongue as if he'd drank Kool-Aid.

"Just like I remembered." He growled as his tongue swept across the back of my neck.

"Get on the bed and get on your knees." He spoke into my ear, and I listened because he had complete control. I grabbed the cover bracing myself for his hard wood only being surprised by the feeling of his tongue sliding in between my lips. My heart started to beat rapidly, and his tongue twisted flawlessly up and down my center. He and I both moaned as he hungrily ate my pussy like it was his last meal. Once his lips squeezed my clit, I yelled his name.

"Fuck, Chill! Shit!" He stopped sucking only for a chance to lick up my juices and go back to my clit. That same motion back-to-back made my body start to shake uncontrollably bringing on an eruption of juices from my coochie. Naturally, my body tried to relax, and he tapped me on my ass with his heavy-ass dick,

"Get back on your knees."

Chill then slammed his dick into my pussy making my head jerk back and my mouth sing his name.

"Chill. Da-Mm." I jerked as he fucked me with so much power and so much passion, I couldn't move a muscle. I closed my eyes so tightly that my nose was scrunched up so I'm sure I wasn't the most attractive person right now. That's okay though. I was taking this dick.

"Fuck baby mama." He sighed without skipping a beat. His hands went from both being on my hips to one pulling my hair. I could no longer control the sounds leaving my mouth. I was howling like a banshee as he moved in and out of my pussy and once again, I started to tremble like a manic. Chill's dick felt so good because it delivered a pleasure nothing else could mimic, pain. As my orgasm started to tighten my coochie around his, he pulled away swiftly and his warm juices dropped onto my ass. I collapsed to my stomach and Chill left the bed, coming back and rubbing a warm wet towel across his spills.

"Now turn around so I can get the front." He directed and I did as he said. I would do anything in the world he wanted me to do right now.

Chapter 6

Chill

My internal alarm woke me up every day at 8:00 am. No matter what time I crashed I was still going to naturally wake up at that time. Getting out of bed, I rocked Tish's small frame, and she opened her eyes one at a time. It reminded me so much of how Noelle looks when she wakes up. I didn't realize how much she was like her mama until now.

"You're leaving?"

"Yeah, I got a little business to tend too."

"Okay, I'll call an Uber."

"An Uber", I raised an eyebrow as I walked into the restroom.

"I'll call my car service to come scoop you up. I'm driving myself around today so it's free to you."

"Okay, that sounds good. Thank you so much."

"No problem. I got you."

I stepped into the hot shower and scrubbed my body with my handmade soap to smell like no other nigga could. Technically no one except my brother who stole a bar anytime he came to my house. Speaking of, I hadn't heard from that Lil nigga since last night. I needed to make sure that fool wasn't in jail.

After scrubbing my body, I rinsed off from head to toe and grabbed a towel to dry off before picking up my phone.

"Siri, call Nick," I held the button on the side of the phone. It rang once and went to voicemail, so I went directly to the jail inmate phone line. As the phone rang, I brushed my teeth and washed my face. It took them like five minutes to pick up, but they were always busy. People do a lot of stupid shit in Vegas.

"Clark county jail."

"Hello, I'm checking to see if my brother Nicolas Saint is incarcerated at your facility."

"Just one second." The line went silent for only a few seconds.

"No Nicolas Saint here."

"Appreciate it."

Once I hung up the phone I felt more at peace. Nick was probably at a hotel with some tourist bitch knocked the fuck out. I walked back into my room and almost drooled seeing Tish standing near the bed with just a red bra and panty set on. The natural curves, the stretch marks on her thighs, and her breasts sitting up nice as hell. She was already attractive before but after fucking her all night I realized my baby mama was the finest.

When she looked up we made eye contact from across the room.

"Why are you looking at me like that Chill?"

"Because to be honest I can't wait to fuck you again." She started to blush.

"When will that be?"

"Shit, I would dick you down right now, but I got important shit to do today."

"Well, there's always tonight."

"You damn right. Until you leave this area code, I'm in that pussy every night."

"Alright, I'm not mad at that baby daddy." She smiled.

Tish got dressed, and she and I both walked into the kitchen. She walked ahead of me switching her thick ass hips flawlessly before she jumped when my housekeeper, Renee caught her off guard.

"Good morning, Tish. It's so nice to see you."

They were familiar with one another because of the constant meet-ups at Dallas airport. I was a busy man, so Renee went to get Noelle for me. I always flew them first class and sometimes sent her in a private plane if I felt like splurging. I trusted Renee with my kid so that meant I trusted her with my life. She was a good lady and always spoke highly of Tish. Apparently, they built a rapport over the years.

"Good morning Ms. Renee, it's nice to see you as well." They gave each other a hug like old friends. Truth be told, these two were probably more acquainted than Tish and me even though we got O.D. acquainted last night. Even standing here I was having flashbacks about how she was throwing that ass back on me last night. Those constant flashbacks were what I had to deal with the last time I had sex with her.

"Where is Noelle?" Renee's eyes lit up.

"She's back in Dallas with my sister. I'm out here on vacation with a couple of my friends."

"Awhn, no Christmas with the baby girl this year?"

"Oh, no worries. I am going back to Dallas in a couple of days."

"That's good, I miss her like crazy. I can't wait to see her."

As she and Renee caught up, one of my cell phones rang from my pants pocket.

"It's Chill."

After a brief moment of indistinct chatter in the background, he spoke up.

"Hi this is Dr. Sean Michaels from Sunrise Hospital and Medical Center. We are looking for Malichai Saint."

"This is him."

"Hello sir, we are reaching out because our patient, Nick Saint said that you were his next of kin."

"I am, what happened!" I raised my voice getting the attention in the room.

"Nick has suffered a gunshot wound and we are treating him here."

Whatever else he was saying I really couldn't hear because my head went blank. Gunshot wound? My brother got shot. I put the phone down. and ran to the key rack to get my car keys.

"Chill, what's going on?"

"The hospital just said Nick got shot." I shook my head still trying to grasp it.

"Oh, my goodness, when? Is he okay."

"I don't know. I'm about to find out though!"

"I'm going with you."

"Me too." Tish and Renee tried their best to keep up with me out the door and down to the lobby. My Benz was already parked out front and I rushed the valet to get my keys.

When we got to the hospital, I asked for his room number, and I must've run the entire way there only stopping to ride the elevator. When I burst inside the hospital room my heart almost skipped a beat until I saw him sitting up in the bed with that big stupid ass smile on his face.

"Boy, you scared my nurse busting in here."

"Bruh? What happened?"

"I got shot at the corner store on Harmon. I'm like the new Tupac." He laughed like something was funny.

"Krys, what you doing here?" Tish spotted her friend who stood at his bedside.

"It's a long story girl. Last night was insane from the time I left y'all until now."

"Yeah, this woman saved my life."

"I wouldn't say all that."

"The Paramedics said you did. Had you not put pressure on my wound I would've bled out."

"Thank God you were there. We should get you back to the hotel to change." Tish put Krystal's hair behind her ear.

"Yeah, I can leave now since y'all are here. I just didn't want to leave him by his self. He just woke up after surgery."

I had to take a seat in the nearby chair because my heart was just now going back to the right speed. I pulled my phone out to call Mrs. Luke from the church to let her know I would be a little late for the Christmas drive. I was supposed to be there in twenty minutes not up here with Nick.

*****

I stayed at the hospital after I sent all the women away just to make sure he was good. Nick is my little brother, but he was my responsibility any time he was around me. Because he always followed me around the world, he was my kid before Noelle. Seeing him in the hospital hurt was doing something to my mind that I couldn't grasp. Parts of me wanted to kill, parts wanted to cry, and parts made me want to pray. I would rather myself be in that bed than him.

When he went to sleep because of the pain meds around 1:30, I decided to leave for the time being. The doctors said he was in a stable condition and besides being in pain he would be alright.

My next stop was Pleasant Grove Baptist Church where I promised to show up for a toy drive. I had never been there for a Sunday service, but I had a decent relationship with the pastor. I met Reverend Moore one night at the airport when he asked to pray for me. Reverend Moore said he saw worry on my face, and he was afraid the devil was winning in my life. Just off of his observation alone, I knew he had a spiritual calling. He was right, and I had a lot on my mind that night. I'd just murdered an old Patna who snaked me over some money. Before then I liked to think I had a poker face when it came to killing. I mean I know I still did; I just couldn't hide it from those spiritually inclined.

When I made it to the church, I found Ms Luke who was running around and fussing at the kids.

"You guys stop running. One of you are going to get hurt!"

She accidentally bumped into me with a pan full of Christmas cookies in her hands.

"Oh, Chill, I'm so glad you made it. I've been trying to keep them entertained as long as I could."

"I'm sorry I was late. Nick got shot but he's okay."

"Jesus Christ, I'm so

sorry to hear that. I will be praying for him."

"I appreciate that. Is the truck that I sent over this morning unloaded?"

"Yes, we have all the toys and bikes lined up in the back. Come on around so we can get started since we're behind a few hours."

I walked into the back of the church and saw all the money I donated was put to good use. There were toys, bikes, books, and rows of Christmas trees with ornaments available for free. A lot of toy drives give away toys with no meaning or thought behind them. I however wanted something with my name on it to be memorable and I know kids would always remember something like getting their first Christmas tree.

With all the riches in the city, Vegas still had poverty in some parts. With run-down Section Eight housing, a high crime rate, and drug use kids oftentimes never had a fighting chance in these areas. Now that I had a daughter, I had a different spot in my heart for kids. When I saw them without, I often thought about if they were my baby. For those same reasons, I did for the youth of Chicago too.

All the people here weren't members of the church but here because of my post on Instagram. There were women here who just wanted to see me and some who actually came for help. Mrs. Luke and the rest of the members formed a line and we began blessing families for the holidays.

"Chill, thank you so much. My babies have been wanting a PS5 since they first came out. You are truly a savior!" I bowed my head.

"I hope y'all enjoy it. Merry Christmas." I handed her a gift card.

"Merry Christmas."

She walked away scooting her kids down the line. Counting the gift cards left in my hand, I didn't look up until I heard my name being called.

"Chill!"

That bitch Monique I fucked in the club last night was standing in front of me in a bright orange long-sleeve dress. I can't lie, I forgot about her ass because Tish's pussy outshined hers like a lightbulb compared to the sun.

"What are you doing here Monique?"

"You posted this event on your Instagram, so I came. I need to talk to you in person about last night."

"I really don't appreciate pop up visits so you will never get that conversation out of me now. Move around."

I attempted to shoo her away. Pressing her lips together she shifted the weight on her foot and stepped up closer to me.

"So, this is who you are? A rich dog ass nigga with money who pretends to be a good person?"

"Monique, you look crazy as hell coming up here. Just go."

"Well, I am crazy Chill. You could've left me alone, but you insisted I come visit you so that you could fuck me and throw me away!" She snaked her neck.

"Bruh shut up. Don't you see we at a church."

"I don't give a fuck! You think I care about how you or any of these other people feel?" She cleared her throat.

"Attention everyone! This man right here is not a good person at all! He invited me to Vegas and to his night club just so he could fuck me and then ghost me!"

"Unht, unht, ma'am you need to leave. We do not speak like this on church grounds."

"I agree, this is not the time or the place for this!"

Two of the elders approached Monique who continued acting a fool.

"No! Y'all need to know who you have representing your church! Chill is a thug and pussy is the only thing he cares about!"

A few members started to force Monique away from me.

"Yeah, his dick may be big but his heart ain't! Stop lying to these people! You a hoe! You a bitch ass nigga!"

If I weren't trying to stay calm, I would slap that bitch in a circle right now. What the fuck wrong with her talking to me like that? Good thing for her we were at a church, and they got her away from me just before I could get mad.

Mrs. Luke came back around the table to continue the giveaway.

"Oh, my goodness. Lord bless her."

"Mrs Luke, I'm sorry she came here with all that. I really just met that girl."

"Baby you don't have to apologize to me. You see all these kids in here getting blessed because of you? If you are indeed blessed below, then of course that kind of stuff comes with it. And let me tell you something, the way she acting, I know it's big and good." She bumped me with her hip and winked her eye. Mrs. Luke lil ass may be an undercover freak, but all of this still wasn't a good look. I be wanting muthafuckas to take me seriously as a businessman and a philanthropist. Now people were just going to associate me with being dick-slanging Willy.

This just proves I have to stop fucking bitches just because I can. Some bitches can't take rejection.

Chapter 7

Dixon

Silent night, holy night
All is calm, and all is bright
Round yon virgin, mother and child
Holy infant, so tender and mild
Sleep in heavenly peace, ooh
Sleep, sleep in heaven, heavenly peace.

Keys and I woke up and he had a bunch of missed calls that sent him into a panic. He rushed me out of the house and down to the lobby where I was sitting waiting for an Uber. My entire body was aching because I'd been put in positions last night that my body hadn't been in since I was a JV cheerleader. With Keys, I had the roughest nastiest sex you could ever imagine. It was nasty in both good and weird ways which left me not knowing how to feel. I mean I like how he licked my ass and ate my pussy. I just didn't like him spitting in my mouth and nutting in my face. Maybe one day I would learn to enjoy freak ass shit like that and not be offended.

As far as the dick, it was phenomenal. It curved like the side of a circle, and I never had that kind before. Plus, he had plenty of stamina, so I was going to need a bag of ice to sit on my swollen coochie lips. I would however take this any day over a nigga who wasn't packing any meat.

My phone alerted me that my Lyft was outside, and I started on my way back to The MGM. The driver didn't talk and that's exactly what I needed right now. Silence to have sex flashbacks.

He let me out in the front of the hotel and then I walked inside bumping into a tall stocky man. When I turned to say excuse me, I saw who it was.

"Leon, where yo ass going so fast?"

"To buy a gun. I been knocking on y'all room door for hours and obviously Krystal up to some bull shit and I ain't having it."

"First of all, slow your roll. How long have you been knocking? Krystal definitely came back last night."

"I know she did, but that don't mean she didn't leave back out. Her phone been going to voicemail all night. Im not stupid."

"Yes, you are if you think Krys would cheat on you. You know she better than that."

"I wish I could be that confident but some sketchy shit going on. Can we at least go check your room to make sure she not in there hurt or some shit."

"Yes, that's fine but calm down. She came back here to meet you. Jumping to conclusions ain't cute."

I walked ahead of him through the lobby. Marching down the gold Italian carpets I got a view of my side profile in the mirror and realized I looked hulled out. I looked and smelled like sex and couldn't wait to rejuvenate in the shower.

Once we got to the doors I went in my purse and realized my room key was missing.

"Damn, I don't have my key. We're about to have to go to the front desk." I griped because I needed that ice and a shower badly.

Walking with these fat coochie lips was making it worse.

When we got to the lobby there was a short line that we waited in for a few minutes before I got to the front.

"Hi, how can I help you?"

"Yes, I lost my room key. Can I get another one?"

"Yes ma'am of course, can we just see your ID please."

I went into my purse and gave her my ID card.

"Room number?"

"632."

She started typing on the keyboard.

"Are you sure it's 632? I'm not seeing your name on the booking."

"The booking is not in my name, it's in my friend's name. Krystal Jones."

"Yes ma'am, but we'll have to see the ID of the person who booked the room in order to issue another key."

"I think she's in the room."

"Well, if she is then we will need to see her ID."

"She's not answering the door."

"Okay ma'am but unfortunately, we are not able to issue out a key. If you feel like she's in any immediate danger, then you may call the police department and go through the steps of a report before we can get involved." She finished and I walked away from the counter.

"That is so dumb. Let me call Tish."

The phone rang a few times and then Tish's phone went to voicemail. What the fuck was up with these hoes.

"Tish not answering either?"

"No, I just text her. I'm sure she will call me back asap." I folded my arms as we stood in the middle of the lobby.

"Look, we can go back to my room and wait until we hear from them, I need a goddamn drink." Leon started scratching his head.

"Okay, the bar right there."

"Fuck that high ass bar, I got a bottle from the liquor store last night. Your friend stressing me the fuck out." Leon complained shaking his head.

"Fine, let's go. I need to charge my phone anyway."

We walked to the Tower One entrance and continued to his room on the first floor. After passing by the high-stakes poker rooms, he swiped his card, and we entered double doors taking us down a long hallway with low ceilings.

"Leon, where the hell are we?"

"Look I didn't have a bunch of money for a fancy room like y'all. I just booked something my pockets could afford with it being Christmas time."

"As long as we don't get mugged back here it's fine."

"Dramatic."

He shook his head as he led us up to his room door. We walked inside and I went straight to his charger I saw plugged into the wall.

"I see you was on a walk of shame just now. So, that's what y'all came out here for?"

"It's not a walk of shame because I didn't do anything. I stayed out partying, that's it."

"Yeah, partying. If you say so." He sat down at the desk and opened his bottle to pour some liquor into a cup. I went through my pictures and videos from last night actually finding most of them embarrassing today. We were fucked up.

"Do you want a drink?"

"Hell no, I'm good until tonight. I need to give my liver a break. I know my stomach is bloated and everything this morning." I got up and walked into the restroom.

Looking in the mirror was my favorite thing to do especially since I got my BBL two years ago. You see I was a chubby girl throughout high school and college so this fine-as-wine shit was new to me. Once I got my first few nursing checks, I put a down payment on my surgery in the Dominican Republic. One year later I was finally getting used to who I saw in the mirror. I felt good.

"Dixon what yo ass doing for new year's, I'm sure you got plans."

Leon had got up from the table and stood at the restroom door.

"I'm going to Atlanta to hang with a friend. What y'all doing?"

"I'm not doing anything and there's not a y'all anymore."

"Leon stop being dramatic, you better hope I don't tell her everything you saying when we find out she innocent. I will snitch."

"You won't."

"How you know?"

"Because I know you can keep a secret."

We made eye contact in the mirror, and he licked his lips. I turned over my shoulder to walk back to my phone and that's when Leon pulled my body in and kissed me on my lips. Pulling away from him I slapped him across his face because what the hell?

"Leon what the fuck is wrong with you?"

"Dixon don't act like that because you all fine now. You had no problem kissing me that night in college." He brought up one of my most kept secrets. Back when my self-esteem was low, Krystal left Leon at our apartment to go to class. While cooking breakfast, he came inside and started flirting with me. At the time, I wasn't used to that attention, so I accidentally played into it and ended up kissing him for at least an hour straight. The whole time I knew it was wrong, but I couldn't stop. Leon was on the basketball team and giving me attention. My fat ass didn't care that he was my best friend's boyfriend.

"I'm leaving. I did not come here for this."

"Please, don't be mad. I just couldn't help myself. I been up all-night stressing and drinking!"

I walked past him so I could get my phone and go out into the casino to wait at the machines or anywhere else that wasn't here.

"Dixon, please don't go. I'm sorry that I offended you. I thought you would enjoy it just as much as me."

"Leon, you are happily married and to my Bestfriend."

"Your Bestfriend but she talks about you every chance she gets."

"About what!"

"About how you're always thinking about yourself and how you be hoeing around. I be telling her to not be so hard on you, but she insists you a bad person. She even judged you for flying all the way to Colorado to have that abortion this summer."

When he said that I knew Krystal must've really been having pillow talk with her husband. I mean, I expected them too but that didn't mean her judgment didn't still hurt. I was at a low point and confided in her about being pregnant. She tried to convince me to keep it, but I couldn't. I wasn't messing up the body I just paid for.

"Whatever Leon. Krystal can think about me what's she wants but that's not going to make me kissing you right."

"Okay, but what about me kissing you?" He started to come towards me again.

"Leon, back up."

"Specifically on your pussy. Would that be wrong?"

"Leon, you need to stop." He pulled me closer and started kissing me on my neck.

"Just let me lick your pussy Dixon. We both had a long day and I really want your ass right now. I have been wanting you, even before all this body. Krystal is snaking both of us, so let's snake her together." I continued trying to push him off, but he was gripping me tighter and tighter. When he pushed me down to the bed I got scared because he wasn't seeming to take no for an answer. Without thinking twice, I kicked him in between his legs, grabbed my phone, and dashed out of the room. I can't believe he was on that type of time. My hands trembled as I walked through the long hallway and out the double doors of the tower. When I hit the corner, I spotted Krystal and Tish going to the elevators. Of course, I would run into them now.

"Dixie, where you coming from?" I contemplated on what to tell them. Telling the truth would come with so much strife. Mentally I wasn't ready for that just yet. I would tell her in due time but right now, I just can't.

"Uh, I'm still drunk from last night. I got lost."

"Girl it's been a long night for the both of us. Krystal saw Noelle's uncle get shot last night."

"Oh my God, what! Are you okay? Did he die?"

"No, he's not dead and I'm okay just a little shaken up. I can't believe seeing the snow globe turned into a night from hell."

"And I thought I had a crazy night." I shook my head. I hugged Krystal and when I pulled away, she squinted her eyes.

"What nigga you been with smelling like Leon's cheap ass cologne? You hooked up with one of them niggas from last night, didn't you?"

I know I should've blurted out what Leon did right in this moment but looking in Krystal's face, I couldn't muster up the courage. I knew telling her would break her heart. It's the holidays and I might not be full of Christmas spirit but taking hers away just seemed wrong. It just wasn't the time.

"Yeah I did. I fucked Keys. The one with the dreads."

"I should've known that would happen from the way y'all were kissing in the club. My friend, my friend." She replied, and right away I started playing back what Leon said about Krystal being judgmental. Maybe I should hold back on telling her everything about my sex life. I'm sure if I did decide to tell her about Leon kissing me, she would just find a way to blame that on my "hoe" ways.

The elevator doors finally opened, and we walked inside. Trying to get the pressure off me I decided to ask Krystal a good question.

"How did you get with Chill's brother last night to see him get shot?"

"So that's the part of the story I hadn't told either one of you yet. When I came back to the hotel, I won sixteen grand."

"What?"

"Sixteen thousand dollars?"

"Yeah, and I only used half of the $243 that I got from Nick."

"How did y'all meet though?"

"When Leon and I got into it in the lobby, I ended up seeing him at the machines. He gave me the voucher, I won, and we ended up together for hours."

"Wow, well congratulations on that friend."

The elevator opened and we got off on our floor. As we walked, Tish started to shake her head.

"Damn, so we all had interesting nights last night."

"Yes, what happened with you baby mama? Did you throw up all over Chill furniture? Your ass was gone."

"No I didn't actually. I more of so came all over his bed for a few hours." Krystal got excited.

"Y'all had sex?"

"We did, and it was beyond amazing. Like I've never in my life felt something hurt me so good."

"Hurt you?"

"Yes, I can't explain it. Let's just say he knows exactly how to fuck with that enormous ass dick."

She smiled as if she was reminiscing.

"Bitch you lucky. Your baby daddy fine, rich, and has a big dick." I replied.

"Leon has two of those attributes but that rich would definitely send him over the top."

Krystal always bragged about Leon's looks because he was a handsome man. He was tall, muscular, with good skin and nice lips which it's sad to say I've felt. His looks were there but it was the father and husband he appeared to be that was attractive. Damn, why did he have to bring up that old guilt I had by kissing me again. I had buried that part of my past a long time ago and respected him as a man. Now I was going to subtly roll my eyes every time she talked about him.

Leon wasn't shit just like the rest of these niggas.

Chapter 8

Krystal

I would probably still be asleep if my phone didn't ring with a call about my children. They were so bad no one would keep them but my mama.

"LJ, how did you knock over your grandmother's tree?" I asked my son who I'm sure was the ring leader.

"Because Faith pushed me, and I fell."

"No I didn't mama, he lying!" My loudmouth daughter spoke up in the background.

"You don't say lying, you say telling a story Faith and y'all are in big trouble when I get home. Mama you still on the phone?"

"Yeah, I'm here."

"Put them in time out for a few hours."

"I'm about to put them in a zoo. They broke all my good ornaments off my tree Krystal?" My mama griped and I felt like I was in trouble too.

"I'm sorry mama but trust Leon is going to handle them when he gets home. Can I call y'all back though? I'm about to get dressed so I can go out to eat with the girls."

"Yeah, I guess." She hung up the phone because she was pissed. I walked over to the restroom sink and started to wipe my face with makeup wipes before applying anything else. The mirror was however fogged up because Dixon felt the need to take yet another shower since we'd been back. I've noticed that she always does that when she's slept with someone she wasn't supposed to. Like she could somehow wash the potential STD out of her.

I wiped the mirror as much as I could and started on my makeup. I didn't wear much and kept it pretty simple since I had good skin and perfect eyebrows. In high school, I thought I would be a model because of my height and my face. My career path didn't end up there, but at least I still had my beauty.

Once we were all done getting dressed, we walked down to the lobby to take pictures with the Christmas tree. I had on some black flare pants, with a white button-up top, and a leather jacket all paired with bright red lipstick. Tish had on a black backless sequence body suit, and red heels, and Dixon wore a leather top, with a pleated shirt, and black fishnet stockings. We all had our style but everyone looked good nonetheless.

"Dixon, can you take my photos because Krystal's tall ass makes me look so short."

I couldn't stand when they brought up my height in a negative light as if I could help it. My whole life I've been taller than everyone and teased about it. Leon was probably the first man to ever swoon over me without feeling self-conscious about me being tall. But I'm sure that's because he was ginormous himself.

When we were done taking pictures, we walked out to our Uber and huddled together because of the cold air. The Uber driver got out and opened his car door inviting us into what felt like a sauna compared to outside.

We rode off towards the Strat and the camera lights had the back seat lit up from all the pictures we were flashing.

"Look who just followed me." Tish said while smacking on her mint fresh gum.

"Nick, aww, I can't believe he even saw my follow."

"He's so sweet with his cute self."

"Yes, Noelle loves him."

I called Nick cute like a child, but I honestly felt that his ass was just as fine as his brother. But because he was almost 8 years younger than me, I had to keep it PG with him. After all, I didn't want to be judged for being attracted to a twenty-one-year-old.

When we got out of the car Dixon started taking pictures of the building from outside. Vegas had so many photo ops we had to keep our phones charged for the memories. As we stood outside, I felt a hand touch my shoulder and when I turned to see, it was my husband with flowers in his hands. He was dressed in a business casual look with a black button-up and jeans. I also saw he's put on the watch I got him for Christmas. It wasn't a real Rolex, but he didn't need to know that.

"For you, my lady." He handed me the bouquet of roses.

"Aww, how sweet." Tish admired them as he handed me the flowers. It was a vase with what looked like two dozen bright red roses the color of my lipstick.

"Thank you, babe, how did you know I was here?"

"You forgot you went over your itinerary out loud every day as you planned it. Tonight is the strat at seven and Oais club at 10:00." He smiled making the corners of his mouth reach his compassionate glare.

"You got it right babe." I pressed my lips together about to get teary-eyed.

"Well, I just wanted to bring you these and apologize for being an ass earlier. I'm leaving back out for California in the morning, so I just wanted to make sure I saw you first. I'm sorry we haven't been getting along and didn't get to spend any time together."

"Well, I appreciate these and I appreciate you coming way out here just to see me. I love you."

"I love you too, and you know I will do anything for you, always."

"Same here." I laid a big wet kiss on his lips.

"You look nice by the way wifey. All of you ladies look nice." He turned to my friends being a gentleman as usual. I loved the brother-and-sister-like bond he and the girls built over the years. My friends loved my husband, and my husband loved my friends. If it weren't for them and their positive affirmations some days, we probably wouldn't have made it this far.

"Alright, I'm about to go. I tipped an Uber to wait for me so that I wouldn't have to call another one. I knew my wife was going to make y'all be on time."

"You know it. But bye baby, be careful."

I held onto his hand as he walked away from me. Leon was dressed nicer than I'd seen him in a while and smelled so good my palms started to sweat. I know I was supposed to be here to eat but I wanted to eat something else. I had a taste for eggplants tonight.

"Ladies, how mad would y'all be if I skipped out on dinner?" I grinned turning to them. Dixon scoffed loudly as she snaked her neck.

"Uh, mad as hell. We're supposed to be eating out together, remember?"

"It's cool Dixon. Let her and her hubby go have a night alone away from the kids. I'm sure me and you can still have fun together tonight."

"Yeah, you right." She rolled her eyes before smirking because she wasn't really mad, she just wanted to be difficult.

"Okay, y'all have fun and don't get too fucked up and do nothing stupid."

"We're not, trust me. Now go get pregnant." Tish smacked me lightly on the ass and I gave both of them a hug. Leon and I then walked down the sidewalk where his Uber was waiting in a Toyota Camry.

"After you, my love." He held the door open for me. When we climbed inside the car Leon took no time whispering sweet nothings into my ear.

"I can't wait to get back to this room. I'm about to make love to your fine ass."

"And I can't wait. You know I crave only you baby."

We started to make out in the back seat. I loved kissing Leon because his lips were so soft, and his tongue wrapped around mine made for an elegant dance. As our tongues deepened, I felt more and more connected to him. Our kisses were like a conversation without words where we could understand each other the most.

The seventeen-minute ride back to the MGM went by quickly because we were kissing so passionately. When we got out of the car Leon was sure to be respectful as always.

"Merry Christmas sir."

"Happy holidays, I know you two can't wait for Valentine's Day."

"And you know it boss."

Leon replied before shutting the door.

"So, my room or yours?"

"Well, me and the girls are in a luxury suite, and we have a nice ass shower we could try out."

"Well let's go."

We made our way up to the room and before we could get through the door, Leon was taking my top off. He took my breast into his mouth only breathing through his nose as he tasted my nipples. He picked me up from the ground and threw me down on the bed as he started to rip my pants off. When my red thong was exposed, he licked his juicy lips and went down in between my legs licking my panties as a tease. When he was finally ready to taste my sweet remedy, he pulled my panties to the side so aggressively that the fabric made a ripping sound. I didn't care because he started eating my pussy like the pro he was. His gentle, slow movements made my pussy drip along with the juices on his tongue.

"You like this baby?" He swirled his tongue around my clit. Leon had good dick, but that mouth always made me squirm.

"Mmhm, you the shit daddy." I started to cum on his tongue. He then crawled on top of me removing his long thick rod and placing it at the entrance of my pussy. Leon pushed himself into me and almost collapsed when he felt how wet I was for him. Leon was my first time, and the only man I'd ever been with, so his sex was all I knew.

"Fuck!" He exhaled before he started to tongue-kiss me. As we kissed, he started penetrating faster and deeper each time his hips rolled. I pressed my long red fingernails into his back leaving scratch marks in my usual spots. The dick was so good, and so powerful until he started to jerk uncontrollably which meant he was about to cum.

To help him out I did a powerful kegal and he exploded nut into my pussy. Thank God for birth control because I didn't want any more kids.

"Damn baby. Give a nigga a minute and I'll get it back up."

"You good baby, whenever you ready I am." I rubbed across his chest.

Suddenly, someone knocked on the door and we jumped up because I figured it was the girls. In a rush, I put on Dixon's cheetah-print robe and went to the door.

When I opened it, an MGM grand worker was standing there with the biggest bouquet of flowers I ever seen. They were ten times bigger than the ones Leon gave me outside the Strat.

"Hi, I'm sorry to disturb you but I have a delivery for Krystal."

"For me, aww thank you." I took the flowers from his hands and shut the room door. I had the biggest smile on my face, and after putting them on the desk I went up to kiss him on the lips.

"Thank you for the flowers daddy. How much did you spend on flowers today?"

"Only the $45 I spent on the bouquet earlier. I didn't buy you these flowers right here."

"Oh, you didn't?"

"No, I didn't, so who are they from?"

"I don't know. I thought you sent them." I started to get nervous.

"We'll just read the card I mean it's right there."

"Maybe they're not for me. Maybe they're for one of the other girls."

"Krystal just read the card and you won't have to say maybe."

"Okay!" I pulled the card from the stake inside the flowers.

"Aww it's sealed, I don't want to mess up their card."

"Krys, it feels like yo ass deflecting and I don't like that. Read the card. Matter of fact, here, I'll read it."

He snatched the card from my hand and started to read it out loud.

"This is a small token of my appreciation and I'm so happy I met yo ass. Last night was mad chill and had I not been with you I would probably be dead. Thank you and enjoy that $16,000. I hope I see you again soon.

Love, Nick,"

"Love nick? You fucking for $16,000. So, you really are a snake ass bitch!"

Leon took the base of flowers and chunked them against the door. He then grabbed my shoulders and shoved me against the wall, pinning my body so that I couldn't move.

"So, you were fucking around on me? That's where you were! With a nigga?"

"No baby I swear. I swear I was not." I whaled so hard I knew my words weren't clear.

"I'm done with you bitch. You hear me? I'm done! I want a mutha fuckin divorce!"

Once he started gathering his things from the floor I went into a full panic.

"Leon stop, please, please! It's not like that. Will you just listen to me? I only went and ate a burger with him and he's thanking me because he got shot and I helped him!" I pleaded, grabbing his arm and he aggressively snatched it back.

"Bitch I said I'm done! I don't care about no excuses you have! Now stop fucking touching me!"

I backed away from him because I knew from his choice of words that he was upset. Of all the years we've been together, Leon has never once called me a bitch before, so I know this was bad.

When he walked out of the door, I fell to my knees and whaled like a baby. The perfect man just walked out of that door and potentially out of my life. I wanted to come to Vegas to live my best life for a moment. Not fuck it up.

Chapter 9

Tish

Dixon and I walked out of the restaurant tipsy as hell. A group of men who were here on a bachelor trip had called us up to the bar and purchased us plenty of drinks. We originally had plans of going back to the room to change but decided to go straight to the club. We'd spent too much time in the restaurant anyway and it was going on 11:00.

"Call an Uber girl, I'm about to call and see how my baby's day was. I miss her."

I stepped to the side to call my sister because she was a night owl, and I knew she was up. When she answered the phone, I heard Noelle crying in the background.

"Bitch, what's wrong with my baby? And why is she still up?" My mommy senses instantly started to tingle.

"She fell down the steps."

"What steps? I know not the steps outside your apartment. Why are y'all out so late?"

"She fell down the last few steps and I was hungry, so we went to Jack in the box."

"Tasha, you took a two-year-old out at 1:00 in the morning."

"Tish, you know I be up all night and I be getting the munchies. Just chill." She sounded like she was high. All I know is the more I think about it, the more I realize I should've probably stayed at home with my child.

"Tish." Dixon got my attention.

"Come on. This is our ride in this white Tesla." I followed her to the car.

"Tasha, are y'all at least inside now?"

"Yes, we are. I'm about to eat and give her these nuggets then we're going to bed."

"Okay, love y'all."

"Love you too, bye."

When we hung up the phone I exhaled because hearing my baby cry made me feel stressed. It was that kind of stress that physically ails you. I was so used to wiping her tears away that I felt like I should be doing it now. When she wasn't away with her father, she was usually with me, and I could protect her from everything. At least I felt that way.

"Tish, you good?"

"Yeah, just worried about my baby again."

"Girl she's fine."

"Is she? My sister is a moron and keeps doing dumb stuff."

"Here friend, let's eat these to calm our nerves."

She went into her purse and then opened her hand in front of me with two vitamin-looking gummies in her hand.

"What is this?"

"They're edible gummies. They supposed to be made with Sativa or something, so we won't be sleepy."

"Yeah, sativa is good to help you stay up." The skully cap-wearing Uber driver butted into our conversation. He looked like he knew exactly what he was talking about giving off a junky vibe.

"Dixon, where did you get those? Them boys from the bar?"

"No, this black girl in the restroom. She was saying how she was scared of heights and coming to the restaurant on top of the world was scary, so she ate these to calm down."

I raised an eyebrow.

"Don't look at me like that. She was a bougie looking black bitch. If she was a cracked-out skater bitch, then yeah this might be meth." She replied and we both started to laugh.

"Dixon you know neither one of us smoke weed."

"But this is not smoking it. It's us having something to mellow us out and enjoy our time tonight. Come on, what happens in Vegas stays in Vegas remember." She raised her cupped hand in the air.

"Okay, whatever, give it here."

"We will just do a half if that makes you feel better."

She happily split the gummy with her front teeth.

"Okay, cheers. May night two be just as wild as night one!"

We chewed the gummies, and I sat calm for a minute waiting for it to kick in. I hadn't felt anything just yet so maybe they weren't strong.

When we got to the club, we walked through the line and this time everything was smooth sailing. The club was playing techno music right now, but they supposedly switched it up from time to time. The scene was however electric, so we made our way through the dance floor. Dixon and I got caught up in the crowd and ended up pumping our fists in the air with a bunch of white people. When a man dressed up as Santa Claus started grinding on Dixon, I took out my phone to record and saw a message pop up from Chill.

Y'all haven't gotten enough of random white boys yet have y'all?"

I jerked my neck back in confusion.

What do you mean Chill?

I wrote back.

Turn around and look up.

When I turned around in a full circle, I spotted Chill's necklace shining in the section up a small flight of stairs. His necklace was dazzling like a disco ball and his teeth lit up the room when he smiled. I unintentionally smiled back at him for a long ass time and then went to text him back. I felt as if I was moving slow as hell though.

I'm starting to think you are following me.

I joked with him.

Nah, you forgot you were in one of my cities? Come up here."

After I read his message, I quickly tapped on Dixon's shoulder.

"Girl, Chill up there."

"For real?" She asked with her eyes enlarged. I started to laugh right in her face because for some reason she looked like a frog to me.

We walked to the section and up the stairs before a security guard in a black suit stopped us. He looked back at Chill who nodded his head, giving us the okay to come in. Right now, it felt like I was walking in slow motion and Chill was drawing me in like a magnet.

"What's up Mama." He licked his lips as he checked me out.

"Hi Chill." I giggled like a schoolgirl.

"Y'all have a seat."

He scooted over on the couch for me to sit.

"Hey, Chill," Dixon spoke to him sounding nervous. This was rare because, since the body change, Dixon had been the most confident woman I knew. I wasn't mad at it because she deserved to be. I saw her when she was low, so being her friend, I loved to see her high.

"What up." He nodded his head at her. He sat back against the couch and looked me up and down as he licked his lips.

"You always dress like this when you go out or is this a Vegas thing?"

"It's definitely not a Vegas thing. I like to be cute any time I'm out having fun."

"MM"

"Do you always rock all these diamonds?" I lifted his chain with my finger. It was much heavier than I expected. He was dressed in a black sweatshirt with a white strip down the sleeves. With the matching black pants, I knew he was in thousands of dollars worth of clothes right now. He looked so damn good that I didn't know what to do.

"Didn't I fuck you in my chain last night."

"Yes."

"Then that should tell you that I don't take them off. Even good pussy can't get them away from me.

"I guess you're right."

I quivered, as I mentally pictured Chill penetrating in and out of my guts. The scent of his cologne made me lean in closer to his body and I unintentionally started rubbing his leg.

"Do you own this club too?"

"Nah, just out-scoping the scene. Checking out my competition. But one day I will. I will own all of them." This confidence in his words was written all over his face. That part of him was instilled in my daughter and I'm just realizing where it came from. She's told me she can do anything she wants in life at the age of two. She's so lucky to have a dad like him because confidence wasn't my strong suit.

"That's goals. I'm proud of you Chill."

"That means a lot coming from you."

He looked me in my eyes, and I felt a rush of his undivided attention. I don't know if it was his eyes or his soul, but something had me in a gravitational pull. The feeling of excitement I felt could be compared to seven Christmas mornings all in one.

"But anyway, y'all get whatever y'all want. We flexing our money tonight."

"Yo boss man. Joseph Gyzer, want to talk to you. Should we let him up?" A guard approached Chill.

"Joseph Gyzer, the nigga from our poker games?"

"Yeah."

"Let that nigga up." Chill didn't move a muscle.

The guards did just as he said like he was the president of the United States giving orders. When the white man in the freshly tailored suit came up the stairs, Chill finally stood up to shake his hand. I couldn't hear exactly what they were saying so I just laid back and relaxed. After all, I felt light as a feather right now.

"Bitch!" Dixon attempted to whisper but she was louder than she thought. I was so caught up in Chill's vibes that I forgot she was even here.

"How are you feeling? I feel like I'm sitting on the top of Spirit flight 826 right now."

"Why flight 826?"

"I don't know. But that's the exact flight I'm on and we're headed to Montego Bay." She darted her eyes back and forth.

"Oh my god! Tish don't move!" She made me jump. She screamed so loud Chill looked over his shoulder.

"Y'all good?"

"No! A big ass spider just crawled on my friend's face!"

"It did?" My eyes got big.

"Yes, bitch it's going to fucking bite you! Get it off!" She made me start to panic. I started feeling the spider crawling over me and really started to panic.

"Oh my God, help me! Get it off! Get it off me!" I started smacking my face and my head. Chill grabbed my arm and shook my entire body.

"What the fuck you talking about Tish? Ain't no spider on you!"

"Yes it is Chill, I feel it!"

"Are y'all mutha fuckas high?" He asked, and I was too embarrassed to say yeah.

"Y'all took drinks from somebody again?"

"No, we ate an edible but fuck that Chill. Help me get this spider off me!"

"Yeah, y'all mutha fuckas high. Snoop go order them something to eat to get this shit off they back."

"What! It's on my back now! Chill help me!"

Chill was shaking his head until he raised his hand and swatted down on my head.

"Alright, I killed it, it's gone. Now just sit back and count to 2,000. Both of y'all." He ordered.

I sat back and started counting and number by number I felt calmer. The last number I remember saying was 107. That's when my eyes started to get extremely heavy and all of a sudden, the club wasn't so loud anymore.

"Tish, wake up."

Chill woke me up with a plate of wings in my face.

"Eat this, mama."

I didn't ask any questions because my stomach felt empty, and these wings smelled good. I dived into my plate inhaling them like I wasn't in the middle of the club right now. Dixon had a plate of her own and she was eating like a pit bull too. This spicy sauce with this blue cheese tastes heavenly.

When I finally looked up from my plate, Chill was standing there laughing. I pushed the plate away and looked around the club having a brief moment of embarrassment.

Chill bent down in front of me and took a napkin from the table before wiping the corner of my mouth.

"You good, everybody has an edible story. I'm about to roll to the casino at the Bellagio for a minute. Y'all rolling with me?"

"Yeah, that's fine. If she wants to go." I pointed to Dixon who was now sucking her last hot wing bone.

"You want some more wings, or you want to go over to the casino with us?"

"Yeah, I'll go."

We all stood up to leave the section and Chill grabbed my hand by surprise. He let me walk in front of him down the steps while placing one of his hands behind my back. His gentle touches and the way he was helping me made me feel something other than just horny around him. I guess I could say I felt safe if you will.

We walked out of the club and got in an SUV, and I sat in the middle of Chill and Dixon. A phone started to ring in the front seat and then the driver handed it to Chill.

"It's Keys." He said in a dry tone.

"What up?" I couldn't hear what was being said on the phone, but I could understand the dynamics of the conversation because of what Chill was saying.

"Bro, come through the casino. That big time real estate agent who sold me my house want to get active at the poker table."

Dixon elbowed my arm and took no time pulling up her camera on her phone and fiddling with her hair. When Chill hung up his phone, he handed it back to the driver.

When our eyes met, he chuckled and started to shake his head.

"What's wrong?"

"'Nothing's wrong. You just beautiful as fuck."

I felt his fingers under my chin turning my face towards him.

"Promise me after we leave here, I get to take you home and fuck you all night."

"I promise. I can't wait.

Jeremiah's song I like, was playing in the background, and we leaned into each other putting our lips in a soft and gentle embrace. We slightly opened our mouths and slipped our tongues against one another. The passion in the car seemed to intensify because my senses were high from that edible. He pulled me in closer and closer until I was damn near on top of him. We didn't stop making out until the car started slowing down and the driver said.

"We're here boss."

I didn't want to stop kissing him but there's always the rest of the night. Thank God we were just getting started.

Chapter 10

Chill

Two hours later

I was up 200 thousand dollars quick, and I was only gambling for fun. To be honest, it wasn't much to me, but it was a quick come-up for a day's work. I was going to add this to my baby's savings account that she already had millions in. One day she would be able to touch all of this money and do with it what she wants long after I'm dead and gone.

Tish and her homegirl were hanging out with me, and she was shocked with the money flying around. When she saw us betting 50 thousand dollars on a hand, she thought we were crazy. But she just didn't know how high the stakes got.

When I would win, she would kiss me on the cheek and cheer like we were at a football game. That shit was low-key cute because Shawty was so innocent and oblivious to this lifestyle.

I hoped this didn't change her mind about putting me on child support. I liked the agreement we had now without putting the court system in our lives. I didn't need any judge telling me what to do and when to do it for my daughter. Tish didn't seem like that kind of person, but you never know how much someone could change over money.

After I played my last hand, I walked up to Tish and her homegirl who were sitting at the bar.

"Y'all ready to roll?"

"Yes.

"Wait, is that Keys?" Dixon asked making me turn over my shoulder. When I spotted him, I saw he was with his baby mama, and I knew shit was about to get messy. Stella was a cool chick at first until she started having that nigga babies and then all hell broke loose. She became greedy and started demanding shit just because she knew she could. Stella was the kind of baby mama that had me scared to have a baby mama. That's why I kept my distance from Tish these past couple of years.

"I know not coming in here with a bitch." Dixon said to Tish who looked at me like I would be the cure to their curiosity. When Keys spotted me standing near these two, he took an alternative route to a blackjack table. I knew he would talk shit about them being with me, but I didn't expect him to be with his bitch. He lived by the slogan; she owned him during the day but at night he was on demon time.

"Girlllllll." Tish dragged out the word which I'm sure had a meaning of its own. I loved the way black woman articulated their words to speak in code that only they could decipher. Shit should be studied.

"Anyway, Chill are you done gambling away your money?"

"Away? Nah mama, I make money. It don't leave me."

"There you go with your cocky ass." She started to bat her eyes. Pretty wasn't the word. I swear I couldn't stop looking at her beautiful eyes and her delicious pink lips. I've never been a kissing ass nigga, but I wanted to kiss her every time I looked at her.

"You still going home with me?

"Of course. Dixon you going back to the room?"

"No, I'm staying here."

"No, I am not leaving you here by yourself."

"I'll Uber to the room."

"You not ubering."

Her and Tish went back and forth.

"Just come to my crib. I'm sure it's nicer than your hotel room anyway."

"It kinda is, I guess that's fine." She shrugged her shoulder going along with the plan.

"Well let's rock ladies. After y'all."

As we walked to the exit door, Keys watched us over his shoulder. Stella noticed him staring and tore her face up immediately. She started snapping her fingers in his face and when he didn't turn around quick enough, she drew her hand back and slapped him before storming off. I laughed to myself because it couldn't be me. I'm 29 years old and never been slapped in my face a day in my life.

We kept walking because I didn't give a damn about what they had going on. Keys and Stella argued and fought every single day.

"Chill, Chill!" I heard Keys calling me from behind.

"Ay bruh, where y'all going?"

"We going to my house. How your cheek feeling?"

"It's alright trust me."

He directed his attention to Dixon.

"But how you doing beautiful. I was hoping I saw you again."

"Wasn't you just in here with your girl?"

"My baby mama. But I'm focusing on you right now love." He wrapped his arm around her shoulder.

The temperature outside had dropped ten degrees since I first left the house. Tish started holding her arms around her waist and chattering her teeth. I wrapped my arms around her small frame to shield her as much as possible. She stopped chattering so loudly and placed her head on my chest like she was comfortable where she was.

"Hey." Keys approached me.

"We're going to get a few drinks at the casino. We will catch up with y'all later."

"Alright, but you better make sure your cat not still on the prowl. I saw her just dock your shit." I joked with him before he flicked me off.

When we got in the car, the driver put on Jay-Z's album The Blueprint

'Cause I see some ladies tonight

That should be hanging with Jay-Z, Jay-Z

(So hot to trot)

Lady

The tension inside the car got too thick to ignore. I knew she wanted me, and I wanted her. Once I looked into her eyes, she gravitated toward me and placed her soft succulent lips on mine. I slipped my tongue into her mouth, and we kissed as I rubbed my hands over her body. We didn't pull away from each other until the driver asked me a question.

"Any stops before the penthouse boss man?"

"No, just get us there quick. You don't need anything do you mama?"

"No, I'm okay. Thanks for asking."

She replied, before kissing me on my cheek.

"Wait." She looked towards me.

"Do you think we need condoms for tonight or you don't care about a slip up?"

"Uhh, I mean I'll pull out. I can control myself mama."

"Okay." She sat quietly for just a few seconds.

"Well can I ask you another question?"

"Yeah?"

"Is this just going to be a sexual thing between us? Or are we working towards getting to know each other."

"Only time will tell. But I am feeling you? I don't think I've been this attracted to a woman in a long time. Shid, since the first time I had you."

She smirked and flashed that one dimple on the right side of her cheek.

"Thanks boo. That's a start, right?"

Her phone started buzzing in his purse and she pulled it out frantically which made me concerned. On her screen was a FaceTime call from her sister and now I was all in because she had my baby calling this time of the night.

"Tasha, is everything okay?"

"Girl yes. Your baby been begging me to call you. She just woke up crying from a bad dream."

She put Noelle in the camera and my heart skipped a beat. Her pretty brown eyes lit up the screen as her long curly hair fell into her face. When she moved it away her little rose cheeks filled the camera and that's when she spotted me.

"Daddy? Mommy is you with daddy?"

"Yes baby." Tish replied, and her sister snatched the phone.

"Bitch what?"

"Tasha, stop cursing in front of my baby and I'll call you later. I promise." They both started to giggle.

"Give me back the phone TT. Mama why you with my daddy and not take me which shoo. I mad!" She crossed her arms and did that little pout that always got her what she wanted.

"Mommy sorry baby. I just ran into daddy on my vacation."

"Hey little Bossy." I called her by her nickname.

"Hi Daddy! I missed you so much!"

"I miss you too baby girl. You being good?"

"Yes." She showed all her little teeth.

"But Noelle, baby you need to go to sleep. Mommy will be home soon to cuddle with you."

"Daddy, are you coming to?" She asked with hopeful little eyes that I hated to take away from her. If I could wrap the world up in a bow and give it to Noelle, I would. It fucked with my mind that I could never actually do that.

"I'll try to baby but get some sleep."

"I love you daddy."

"And I love you."

"I love you too mommy. I love you and daddy. I can't wait to see y'all!"

"Okay." Tish smiled and her voice cracked because Noelle had touched her heart too.

When she hung up the phone I kind of felt bad that I had lied to my baby. It wasn't that I couldn't go see her, I just didn't let it cross my mind. I know even with the agreement I could go see my baby more especially around the holidays. It truly shouldn't matter what the schedule says, and her mama and I need to work on that.

Once we got to the Palms, we went up the elevator to my floor.

"Can I use the restroom."

"Yeah, it's one back here in my bedroom. Come on, make yourself at home."

When she went into the restroom, I heard my shower come on and her closing the glass door. I loved a woman with good hygiene and made sure to always be clean around me. That honestly just brought out the freak in me even more. I've never actually run into dirty pussy, but some bitches don't care as strongly as others, and I will never eat day-old pussy.

I sat on the side of the bed and took off my jewelry placing it into my jewelry box stashed under my bed. I liked to lay on top of it so I could protect my riches like a king in his tomb. There were tens of millions of dollars of jewelry under me and what's crazy is I still want more.

"Chill. Come here for a second." Tish yelled from the restroom. I figured she just needed help with the faucets until I walked inside, and she was standing naked.

"Do you want to join me? I found this in there and it looks interesting." She held a small whip in her hand. I had that one night I was with a freak I met at Oasis nightclub. She was into that BDSM shit and wanted me to do all types of shit with her. She could take a lot; she just couldn't take this dick. Only one bitch could, and I was looking at her right now. Damn near drooling staring at her bald pussy.

I didn't respond verbally and just took off my clothes to join her. She had the water temperature up high so the glass around the shower was full of steam.

I kissed her on her lips and then I squeezed her hips before twisting her around to face the glass. The water from the shower heads was pouring onto my face but I kept my eyes open because the burn didn't bother me.

I smacked her ass with my hand.

"You sure you want to go on another level with me tonight?"

"I want to go wherever you take me, Chill." She sounded as if she was biting her lips. I bent down behind her and kissed her ass cheeks before pressing my teeth into her skin. Oh, girl from Oasis told me women who like pain don't just like it, they love it. I licked my tongue up the slit of her pussy and then stood up to see how much of the dick and whip she could take. I pushed myself inside of her and just as she gasped, I took her breath away again smacking her with the whip.

"Fuck!" She cried out.

"This what you wanted right?" I started to stroke my dick into her guts. I smacked her ass with the whip again and again as my waistline clapped against her cheeks. She was taking that dick like a pro and staying right in the place like I wanted her. Her pussy was already wet too. She liked this shit.

"How you want it mama?"

"Harder baby, harder!" She grabbed her breast only balancing herself with one hand against the glass. When I looked down and my entire eleven inches had disappeared inside her I felt myself start to nut and I had to pull out.

"Fuckkkk." I grunted, and she grabbed my dick trying to put it back into her pussy.

"Wait, this mutha fucka cumming mama."

"I know, but I want you inside of me. We can deal with that tomorrow, just don't stop."

She started throwing her ass back on my dick and I held the wall behind me trying not to moan like no bitch, but it didn't work. Tish had me in here singing like Luther.

Chapter 11

Dixon

11:00 am

I rolled over in the crisp white sheets unaware of the time. In my stomach was an uneasy feeling as if water and food were bubbling up. When I sat up on the side of the bed, Keys turned over to position himself in the other direction. I tried to hold my lips together but unfortunately, I still felt like throwing up.

Jumping up from the bed I ran into the restroom and began puking my insides out. When I got a chance to breathe, I sat on the floor beside the toilet and the Rio hotel sign caught my eye. That's the only reason I knew my location. All I could smell on my breath was Hennessy and as I sat there, memories slowly started to come back from last night.

Keys and I started at the casino bar and drank up a very large tab. Then we went to the Walgreens on the Strip and got a bottle of Hennessy. The last thing I remember was sucking his dick in the back of an Uber under his jacket. After that, everything else was just a blur. Maybe I will remember more as the day goes on.

I got up from the floor and spit into the toilet once more to get that taste out of my mouth. After wiping it with a wash rag from the counter I went to wash my hand.

"Where the fuck did this come from?" I twisted around a ring on my finger that was slightly too big. It was placed on my ring finger on my left hand and that quickly made me raise an eyebrow.

Shooting out of the restaurant I went to grab my phone to see if I had any missed calls. After Face ID unlocked it, I scrolled through meaningless messages as I climbed back into the bed. The first place I wanted to check this morning was Snapchat. Hopefully, I collected footage of my night to have some type of documentation.

As I knew, Snapchat was going to tell me the whole story since I was a content creator even while drunk. Keys and I took lots of pictures from the casino to the famous Las Vegas Nevada sign. I closed my screen and pouted when I realized I had to get out of this bed to grab the open bottle of ginger ale on the table. I was still coherent enough to know I would need this for my hangover. Standing in the middle of the room floor freezing, I gulped down the ginger ale until I spotted a holiday-themed packet that read One Love Wedding Chapel. Once I opened it and read the first page my heart dropped. It was a wedding certificate. Keys and I got married last night. What the fuck.

"Keys, Keys, wake up nigga!"

He started to groan.

"Damn. What the fuck wrong with you? You supposed to wake a nigga up with some head or something."

"Keys did we get married last night? Or is this a joke?"

He rose from the bed and took the folder from my hand.

"Damn. Here I was thinking this shit was just a dream."

"Well, it's not, so we need to fix this ASAP. I barely know you!"

"Okay, we can, calm down. It's nothing an annulment can't fix." He brushed his long dreads out of his face.

"We need to get on this ASAP because I leave in the morning."

"And we will." He scrunched up his face.

"But on the cool you starting to offend a nigga, acting as if you marrying me is the worst thing in the world."

"I never said it was, but this was not planned. I'm still trying to remember when it happened."

"Shit me too. I guess them bottles we popped last night, popped us in return."

"Tell me about it." I crossed my arms and dropped my chin to my chest.

"So you going to sit there and pout all day of you going to come and give your husband some love?

"My husband?"

"Yeah, your husband, fuck you mean? Until we go to that chapel for the annulment you officially Mrs. Xavier Keys."

"You're joking right?"

"Yeah, but only for a while. You should lighten up too. Playing house for the day won't be so bad."

When Keys finally got up from the bed his dick was so large in his boxers that I could see the brim of the head. Looking eye to eye with that made my mouth water and one thing I couldn't deny, was that he is fine.

"Why are you looking at me like that? You bout that action or you melodramatic?"

"You already know how I get down. Don't play."

"Well prove it."

"Come here!" I shrugged my shoulders with a confident smile across my face.

"Shit, say no more." He grinned while rubbing his hands together. I took out his dick and put it in my mouth touching the back of my throat. With my hands by my side, I started gulping his dick like a Pepsi on a hot summer day. His thick, heavy penis was sliding on my tongue making me feel as if I had complete control of him now. With my head bobbling as fast as it could he started to cum so hard, he squeezed the top of my head like a ball. I had no choice but to swallow his semen because he'd put so much inside my mouth. I smiled while looking up at him and smacked my lips.

"Damn. I don't care what you say. You wifey for today. Now go get dressed. That nut got me hungry." He bent down to stick his tongue deep down my throat. I guess I could play along for a few hours.

We got dressed in our clothing from last night and used the toothbrushes and soaps provided by the hotel. Keys Bentley was parked in the nearby garage and when we got inside, we laughed at my panties being left in the seat.

"I wonder how many times we fucked last night; I know my heart rate was up." He laughed while shaking his head.

"Yeah, and mine too. It's just exercise. It won't hurt."

"Yeah, you got that right wifey." He winked his eye at me. Looking at Keys in the daytime made him finer in a way. The true chestnut color of his complexion simmered like gold dust in the sunlight. I also noticed that his sideburn had been replaced with the word Humble vertically down the front of his ear. Keys being a deadhead, he wasn't my usual type, but he was changing my opinion one stroke at a time.

"I hope you like brunch because there's this fire place I go too almost every morning."

"I'll take anything right now, I'm so hungry," I replied, stroking my hand down the side of his face. There was something so right about being here with him right now and I couldn't explain. I guess because it's been a while since a man wined and dined me unapologetically. Most men even Tish's daddy never took me out. They always wanted to lay up and do nothing productive for the day.

It took us only fifteen minutes to get to the brunch spot locked in a strip center. When we exited the car, keys met me at the trunk with his hand extended out. He kissed me on my cheek and then we started towards the front door. Keys soon smacked his lips looking back at the car.

"I have to go back to the car to get this out." He left my mind wondering what 'this' exactly is.

"What did you need to get?" I asked when he approached me.

"Oh, just this bottle of pills out the car."

"Damn, you turning up this early?"

"Nah." He smirked.

"This is my heart medicine. I have to take it every day. I've had heart surgery a few times since I was a kid.

"Oh." I was left with no words for the time being.

"Yeah, I know I seem too young to have them type of problems, but I do. My dad and my brother died young, so I try my best to prevent it and take this shit to survive." His jaw twitched a bit as he started to reminisce.

"Well, that's good that you're staying on top of it. Heart problems are very serious."

"Tell me about it." He held the door as we approached it. Though Keys had something as horrible as a heart defect everything else about him seemed to be perfect. From the way he paid attention to me, to the sheer thug demeanor he displayed. I could get used to him and the feeling he's giving me right now. Pretending to be married was fun so far and I was going to enjoy it while it lasted.

Chapter 12

Krystal

I stood at the door of my hotel room, debating on if I wanted to go or not. Being stuck in this room alone and being ignored had me thinking unnecessarily and recklessly. My Uber was outside, and I still didn't know if going to the hospital was a good idea. I didn't want to party, I didn't want to gamble, I just wanted to talk to someone easy to talk to.

I pulled out my phone to dial Leon's number for one last time. The phone didn't even ring before I heard the voicemail prompt. I smacked my lips and hung up the phone hoping my nonchalantness would kick in sooner or later.

Fuck it, imma just go. I pumped myself up and left out of the door.

When I got downstairs and into the Uber, I texted the girls that I would be back in the room soon. I didn't specify where I was going, and I was praying I didn't run into either one of them there.

It took us about ten minutes to get to the hospital. When I reached the front desk, I told them I was coming to see Nick Saint, and they told me the room number. Once I reached his hallway, I spotted a nurse coming out of his room laughing as she held her stomach. Even in pain, he was managing to make people laugh. That's the reason I needed to be here now. I knew he would lift my spirits as he did two nights ago.

Walking into the room I was confused about where he was until I saw him being helped out of the restroom and back into his hospital bed.

"Krystal, the thousandaire, I'm surprised to see you here."

"I know I should've called before I came but I just wanted to stop by before I leave tomorrow. You doing okay?" I asked as I sat down in the chair next to his bed. The room smelled just like his cologne as if it was seeping from his skin. It wasn't a strong scent but just strong enough to take over my senses for the moment.

"I'm alright. I'm as good as I can be with my ass out. Where your home girls?"

"Somewhere running around the city. We honestly see each other more in Dallas than we have here."

"Vegas will do that to you." He laid his head back on the pillow looking up with a vacant stare. I didn't know much about Nick, but I did know about people and body language just from being a teacher. I can always tell when a student is having a bad day just by the slightest droop in their shoulders.

"Physically, I know you're fine but mentally are you okay?" I broke the silence that had settled over the room.

"To be real mentally I'm a little fucked up. It seems like every time I try and do good, I take ten steps back. I was just starting to get my Christmas spirit too. That's why I invited you to the sphere. The past few years I been ignoring the holidays since my grandma died the day after Christmas."

"Damn, I know that was rough. My grandma died on Easter morning a few years back."

"Man, I know that's hard too. You probably hate boiled eggs, don't you? Does seeing bunny's and carrots and shit make you sad?"

He had a serious look on his face, but I couldn't help but laugh.

"No silly, I just hate the feeling I get when I think about it is all. I didn't allow myself to hate the holiday just because of what happened with her." I took a brief pause.

"Hey, what if I know something that can help bring your spirit back a little?"

"Like what?" He flashed a wide grin and raised his eyebrow.

"Like a Christmas tree in your room. I mean, since you may be here on Christmas Day, we should make it feel like Christmas in here."

"And how are you supposed to do that?"

"You will see, just give me about an hour." I rose from my seat and threw my purse over my shoulder. I walked to the door, and he stopped me just as I grabbed the handle.

"Wait, where you going?"

"I'll be back."

I said, before walking out of the door. As I made my way to the lobby I pulled out my phone and requested an Uber to a Walmart about eight minutes away. The Uber driver pulled up blasting Jhene Aiko and from there I knew it would be a peaceful ride.

When I got to the Walmart I ran inside, grabbed a basket, and started filling it with all the decorations I could find. I got a small five-foot Christmas tree, two containers of ornaments, and a star to place on top. For what I was doing, I didn't need much. My tree at home was however covered in thousands of ornaments. Being in the Christmas spirit I bought them for years and had never thrown any away.

"$92.11" the cashier spoke, and I slid my card with ease. I still had a $16,000 check so money felt indispensable to me at the moment. I walked out of the store and tipped the driver who waited on me.

"Thank you, ma'am, do you need any help?"

"No, I got it. I'll just grab a wheelchair from out front."

I pulled a wheelchair over to the trunk and started to unload it. After unloading all my things, I strolled my items into the hospital. The lady at the security desk was looking at me with a curious scowl but she never said anything to me, so I kept going up to his room.

"Knock, knock." I spoke, coming back into the room. Nick smiled and licked his lips before making a joke out of me.

"Is that a handicap Christmas tree?"

"No silly, I just needed something to bring it up here. I'm about to put it up for you. Which corner do you want it?" I started removing the tape from the box with my hand.

"Over there by the window. That's where my mama always put them."

A dimpled smile came across his face and I went to work. I put the tree up, fluffed the fake pines, and even turned on Christmas music on my phone. Every time I looked towards Nick he was smiling, and his joy was lightening my mood.

"Damn, you really doing all this for me."

"Of course. You still in shock?"

"Hell yeah, nobody I deal with on a regular basis would think of doing no shit like this, so thank you."

"You're welcome, Nick, it's no problem." I replied and he flashed a one-sided smile. We were making eye contact so long it started to get hot in the room, so I took off my jacket. I tried focusing on the tree and taking my mind off the look Nick had just given me.

After I placed the last red bulb on the tree, I backed away to check out my work.

"All done. What do you think?"

"It's a masterpiece." He made me smile.

"Oh, and I like the tree too. Come here for a second."

I walked over to him just as nervous as a teenager on her first date or better yet her first time.

"Nah, you can sit right here with me." He stopped me as I squatted over the chair. I sat down on the bed beside him and was too scared to look his way because I felt sexual tension next to him. He finally grabbed my chin and made me turn his way and came in toward my face. His eyes were lowered, his mouth was slightly ajar, and the scary part was that my expression was the same way.

"Nick, I shouldn't."

"Shhh." He stopped me placing a kiss on my lips. He followed with another peck and then another until our tongues were intertwined together. The warmth from his breath caressed my lips and made my body start to shiver. After I allowed him to kiss me for some time, I pulled away from him.

"I can't do this, I shouldn't. I should just go." I got up and scrambled to collect my things. Nick was saying something to me, but I refused to stop and listen. I was making mistake after mistake out here in Vegas and not making anything in my life better.

I caught a ride back to the hotel room and dashed straight to the room. When I placed my key up to the door, I heard my girls laughing and I was happy they were here.

"Hey Krys. Me and Dixie were just saying we probably weren't going to see you anymore this trip since you were booed up with hubby last night."

"Unfortunately, I haven't been booed up because hubby gone. He left last night and said he's getting a divorce."

"What? Was this before he sent you that big-ass bouquet of flowers?" Dixon asked, pointing at the flowers that started this big mess.

"Those flowers came from Nick which made him think I was cheating."

"Is he crazy?"

"Not really, I just made him right by kissing Nick at the hospital about thirty minutes ago."

When I confessed to that, they both went silent, and I sat down on the bed.

"Damn, friend." Tish started rubbing on my back. Just that physical touch and her sympathy made me start to ball. My hands were shaking, my breathing started to pick up, and I felt a strong panic attack coming on.

Dixon kneeled in front of me and started rubbing my forearm.

"Krystal, breathe. You are way too worked up right now."

"I can't help it. I fucked up so bad. I lost my husband because I was being stupid. How could I fumble such a perfect man because of a Christmas trip."

"You did not fumble him Krystal and he's just mad because he thinks something happened. You don't have to tell him about that kiss." Tish replied, with a sad smile on her face.

"Yeah, I agree with Tish. Don't tell him about the kiss and deny that shit until you're blue in the face."

"But Dixon we don't lie to each other. Leon and I tell each other everything and he would never deceive me like that. I had no business going to that hospital in the first place. I should've been chasing my husband. I wish I would die."

I dropped my head to the floor after confessing my suicidal thoughts. The room was the quietest it's been since we been here but I didn't regret what I said. It was true, I felt low, down, and the complete opposite of my usual cheerful self.

The only thing that could be heard in the room was me crying until Dixon cleared her throat before starting to talk.

"Krystal, you know I love you and I never what to see you in pain. But truth is, Leon is not as perfect as you may think. Don't threatened to kill yourself over him."

"What does that mean?" I scrunched my face up.

"It means don't sweat what you did because as I just said, Leon is not perfect."

"Okay but why are you saying that?"

"Look, I know you may not want to hear it and trust it's hard for me to say but," she took a long pause.

"Leon tried to kiss me yesterday. I saw him in the lobby, and we went back to his room to wait on y'all to open the door."

"Wait a minute, what?" I jumped from my seat and gritted my teeth.

"Calm down Krys and sit back down."

"Calm down? Sit down? Dixon did you not hear what you just told me. My husband tried to do what with you?"

Tish grabbed my arm because she knew I was mad enough to fight right now.

"I'm telling the truth. He tried to kiss me to get back at you and I wasn't having it. I'm only telling you because I don't want you beating yourself up for doing you."

I grabbed two handfuls of my hair and pulled them as hard as I could. I let out a loud screech and glared at Dixon like she was red, and I was a bull.

"Why are you just now telling me this! If you're my friend, you should've said it when it happened!"

"I didn't want to hurt you, Krystal! You think that man is perfect and I ain't want to spoil your happiness."

I started pacing the floor because my body wouldn't allow me to continue standing still.

Tish attempted to hug me but I pulled away from her too because I didn't know who I could trust. Dixon was a known hoe but one thing she hadn't been proven to be was a liar. The only problem is a known hoe means she could've done something to provoke him. This could all be her fault.

I grabbed my coat and then stormed towards the door with Tish following behind me.

"Krystal, where are you going? You need to sit down and breathe."

"No, I need to go outside and breathe. I just need some air after all this. I'll be back, I just need some air."

"Okay, I'll go with you."

"No! I just want to go by myself. I want to be by myself right now."

Tish pressed her lips together tightly and then let go of her grip on my arm. I stormed out of the door shooting through the halls until I got in front of the big lion placed in the middle of all those presents. I stopped to call Leon's phone because I just couldn't hold it in any longer and I needed to talk to him.

"The number you have called is not accepting calls at this time."

I hung up and called again but the same message started immediately. He must've changed his number.

"Fuck him! Fuck him." I yelled at my phone and realized I looked crazy, so I walked outside. When the fresh chilled air hit me, that still didn't help and now I was just cold and mad. That's when I realized the only way I could get passed this was to take my mind off him completely. And what better way than going back to where my heart was racing for another reason?

I called an Uber and with the high surge of drivers; I was quickly picked up and back on my way to the hospital. Now that I'd been here twice in the past day, I knew exactly how to find him without following signs or checking in. When I walked into his room, he was sitting up on the side of the bed looking out the window.

"Hi, Nick."

"What's up. You forgot something?" He lifted an eyebrow.

"No, I just got in a car and came here because I didn't know where else to go."

"You surely knew where when you ran up out of here after I kiss you."

"I'm sorry Nick. It wasn't that I didn't enjoy it. I was just torn."

"Between what?"

"Doing what's right and doing what my body wanted to do." I twiddled with my thumbs. I was so nervous, but I knew exactly what I came here for this time.

"Mm, well it's your world baby. I'm just a squirrel trying to get a nut." He turned back to the window.

"What if I'm a squirrel trying to give you a nut."

When he turned and looked back towards me his smile spread across his face, but his expression told me he was confused. Without further explaining myself I walked to his bed and squatted down in front of him. The gown he was wearing made it convenient for me to access his dick. He still had a gunshot wound so I was careful of where to place my arms. I didn't have to lean forward much because his long caramel stick was already sticking out towards my mouth. I started gobbling his dick up and that's when I heard the sexiest moan I'd heard in a while. Leon didn't ever let out his moans which was annoying and uninspiring when I thought about it.

"Fuck, baby! Eat that dick."

He encouraged me, making me go even further. While I gave him head, I rubbed my hand over my pussy to get myself nice and juicy. When he saw what I was doing, he grabbed my arm and put my fingers up to his mouth. He licked the cream like it was an ice cream cone and then let me put my fingers back on my pussy. I had his dick so hard, and soaking wet it seemed to glisten against the light in the room. Nick was blessed below, and I was quite shocked because he was younger.

When I stood up from the ground, I pulled down my pants and turned to face the window and ride him cowgirl style. I stood over the thigh that hadn't been injured and slowly bounced up and down. He put his forehead against my back and started caressing my breast so sensually. He was filling me up with so much dick I wanted to scream his name but inside here. I knew I couldn't.

Covering my mouth with my hand I felt I was in control until he lifted my shirt and started kissing me on my back. I didn't know it before, but I had plenty of spots back there that I didn't know about, and he was touching them all. My body started to shake, and my pussy started to flow right as Nick reached around and grabbed the front of my neck.

"Cum down this dick and don't stop until I tell you too. Come on. Nut for me."

I did just as he said and had the longest hardest orgasm, I think I ever had. My stomach muscles contracted, my clit felt like it was vibrating, and my pussy didn't want to let go of Nick's dick.

"Ahh Ahh Ahh. Didn't I tell you not to stop until I tell you to? Come on baby I got stamina. Don't think this gunshot graze stopping that." He smacked the top of my ass. Usually after an orgasm Leon and I took a nap but now I get to have another one. At least I was ending my time in Vegas with a bang. Or a thang, a really big one.

Chapter 13

Tish

Last night in Vegas

After that big blowout in the room I too needed some fresh air. The wind outside was cold, and the temperature was almost in the 40's which would normally be weather I avoided. Tonight, it however felt good to my skin, but I think that's because I wanted to somehow numb the pain. My two best friends being at odds just didn't sit right with me. Ever since college we'd all been thick as thieves and depended on one another. I remember back in college we wouldn't eat without one another. I would starve for two whole hours just to meet them in the café for lunch. There were also other times when we had each other's back even more than having lunch together. One time Krystal got jumped in the restroom at a party and we spent the whole next week looking for the girls that did it. We never found out who they were, rumor was they were some local bitches that crashed our college event. That's however when I realized we were more like sisters than friends. Neither one of us had ever fought Dixon but we were all ready to go to war for one another.

    Looking at the New York New York hotel across the street, I took a moment to admire the beautiful Christmas lights across the roof. I pulled out my phone and took a few pictures before I started down the sidewalk.

I was nowhere near alone walking out here despite the weather. The sidewalks were crowded, and the smell of weed was overpowering out here. I didn't make it far from the hotel when I decided to turn around and just sit on a bench outside the hotel for a while. It was way too crowded out here tonight.

"Merry Christmas beautiful."

A man said as we passed one another.

"Same to you," I replied, walking in the opposite direction. More and more men started saying stuff to me and one stopped to talk but thank God my phone rang. When I saw who was calling I smiled brightly and hurried to push accept.

"Hey."

"Hey mama, where you at?"

It was something about the way he called me Mama that turned me on.

"Walking down the strip."

"Oh, we'll I didn't mean to interrupt y'all time. Y'all be careful."

"It's no y'all, it's just me. I needed to get out of the hotel for a minute. The tension with my friends is really high."

"Ain't that normal though? Don't females usually get into it on girls' trips."

"That's never been us though. I'm afraid this argument is much worse than a small disagreement."

"Damn, I hope they get it together." He paused.

"But hold on, you out by yourself?"

"Yeah. I'm walking halfway down the strip."

"Nah mama, I don't like that. You don't need to be out alone. Vegas is nice to look at, but foul shit be going on all the time." His voice seemed sterner than it was before.

"Okay, you're right. I should turn around."

"Yeah, go and wait in the lobby. I want to come pick you up and bring you something."

"Something like what?"

"A Christmas gift."

I couldn't help but feel my knees buckle when he said he got me a gift. Maybe he was just talking about his penis but that was still a good thing. I was quite fond of that.

"Okay boo, I'll head and wait in the lobby."

"Alright. I'm on my way." He replied before hanging up the phone. I turned on my heels and walked the other way with a much quicker strut. I couldn't wait to be in his presence again. That was just what I needed.

When I got to the lobby, I waited only twelve minutes before he was telling me he was outside. I walked out and met him in an all-white Rolls Royce parked outside. The valet attendant opened the coach doors and I climbed into the front seat admiring the orange leather interior. When we pulled away from the hotel Chill had smooth jazz music playing which through me off. I didn't take him for that type of guy.

"Your musical choice is impressive. I love this type of music."

"Oh yeah? This is Ornette Coleman. He's a great saxophonist. My pops used to listen to him after dinner back in the day. Jazz music really keeps me calm."

"Yeah, and you seem too always be calm. Your dad passed away a while ago, right?"

"Yeah. Brain cancer. In 2006." He cleared his throat because I could tell he was getting uncomfortable. I hurried to try and think of something to change his mind. It however seemed that under pressure I couldn't come up with anything other than,

"So where are we headed Noelle's dad?"

"Don't worry, just sit back and enjoy the view. We will be there in about twenty minutes." He looked towards me and smiled. As he drove towards our unknown destination, I sat wide-eyed in the passenger seat. Just as Chill said, it took about twenty minutes to reach our location. The Green Valley Ranch Resort sign shined brightly at the entrance as we pulled in. All of the trees were illuminated from the thousands of bulbs wrapped around them.

"This place is so nice. What are we doing here?" I asked, interrupted by the valet attendants opening our door.

"Mr. Saint, it's nice to see you on site today. I am here to make you and your beautiful guest as comfortable as possible."

"Thank you." Chill stuck his hand out.

"Can we get an igloo tent please."

"Of course, sir. Right this way."

The way they were treating Chill let me know he either owned this place or frequented here a lot. I wasn't surprised by what Chill had anymore. He honestly seemed to have it all.

We walked down a winding path of lights mixed in with the nature surrounding us. I was walking with my head on a swivel just to take in it all. Once we reached the end of the pathway there was a white sign displayed which read, Christmas on The Terrace. Straight ahead of us, we're sculptures lined side by side all meant to look like glass igloos. It was beautiful and so magical I got the chills. I couldn't believe I was here in the flesh.

When the hostess took us to the furthest igloo on the pathway we walked inside where there was a table, chairs, and a beautiful rug on the floor.

"Have a seat mama." Chill pulled out a chair for me.

"This place is so nice Chill. How did you find it?"

"One of my poker buddies owns a share in the resort. I used to stay here anytime I came to Vegas before I purchased my penthouse. It shits on them hotels on the strip if you want peace."

"Yes, it does. Our daughter would for sure love this igloo."

"Man." He shook his head after sitting in his seat.

"What's wrong? Why did you say that?"

"You saying our daughter just does something to me. I guess it's because I'm finally around someone who I can say loves her just as much as me."

"Yes, and we're bonded for life because of that. Whether we originally wanted it or not."

"Thank you for everything you do Tish. For real, you been about peace and her well-being since she been here. I know she safe with you and that takes a lot off my shoulders."

"I'm glad you feel that way, and I hope we could love her together one day and not love her apart."

"Yeah. We gone make it happen. That's a promise, I'm kind of hooked on you."

He smiled and licked his lips before he leaned into my body. After grabbing my chin, he placed his moistened lips onto mine and slipped his tongue into my mouth.

He held my chin as our tongues danced to the beats of our hearts. This made me want even more of him.

We stopped kissing just in time for the waiters to come and take the order for our drinks. We both ordered spiked hot chocolate and it came back to us pretty quickly. This hot chocolate was the best I've ever had, and I truly tasted no alcohol.

I sipped the whole cup so quickly I started to feel kind of dizzy.

"Whooo."

"You alright?"

"To be honest, I'm drunk off that one cup." I giggled as he chuckled at me while shaking his head.

"Lightweight. Do I need to feed you wings again?"

"No. I would much rather have something else in my mouth. It's way bigger than a wing though."

I winked my eye at him.

"Well shid, let's go. We ain't got nothing but, 12 hours until your flight anyway." He looked at his watch.

"Well lead the path, after you."

"Damn okay. I was going to feed you but."

"Just feed me that dick." I made him smile. We both stood up and rushed to leave the igloo. As pretty as it was, we had something even more beautiful in mind.

Once we got back to the front, Chill didn't have to say a word and we stood there waiting for the car to pull back up. The warmth coming from Chill's body was the only thing keeping me warm right now. This 40-degree weather felt more like a cozy campfire. I rested my head on his arm until the car pulled up and we climbed inside. The same calm chilling music started to play, and chill turned the music up so loud it vibrated through my entire body. It wasn't in a rattling way but kind of like a full-body massage. I wanted to close my eyes to enjoy it a little more.

When Chill and I turned off the highway he pulled into a gas station.

"You need something? Water, juice, sweet ass soda?"

I shoved him in his head playfully and he laughed it off.

"You better be glad I want to fuck you all night."

We laughed as he climbed out of the car. As soon as his second foot touched the pavement, I saw a silver barrel come out of nowhere. My heart skipped a beat as Chill started to slowly raise his hands.

"Give me everything you got in here. You got it don't you rich ass nigga." He tugged at Chill's diamond-studded chain.

"Say, don't touch me bum ass nigga."

"Shut the fuck up before I smoke you and my homie smoke this bitch." I looked to my left and spotted a second gunman at the passenger window. I started to panic, my breathing became heavy and instantly my mind went into a prayer.

"Just get what you niggas want."

"Nah you give it to us. Give it up."

"Yo, Rhino, you want me to take her shit too."

"Nigga shut the fuck up!"

You could tell he wasn't supposed to say his name.

"Give me your gun because I know you got one on you and all these diamonds too nigga! I'm not playing with you!"

Chill took off all his jewelry and gave it to them and they ran off behind the store.

"Fuck! Fuck!"

Chill punched his steering wheel so hard I'm sure his knuckles were bleeding.

"Should we call the police?"

"What the fuck is the police going to do?"

"Why are you yelling at me Chill! I'm just asking!" I yelled back and he slammed his door. Chill sent his tires screeching across the parking lot leaving smoke behind his car. I put on my seat belt and tried to slow my heartbeat down because it was almost thumping out of my chest.

We drove a little way as Chill gripped the steering wheel tightly with the veins in his hand protruding.

"Where are we going Chill?"

"I'm taking you back to the hotel. I can't be around you anymore."

"What the fuck did I do? I didn't have anyone come to rob you, Chill. Is that what you think?"

"Hell no. I just know had I not been with you them niggas wouldn't have gotten shit from me alive. They would've had to kill me first."

"Why would you say that Chill! You have a daughter to live for."

"Yeah, and without you she won't have nobody. That's why we can't be around each other. As you can see, shit ain't just peaches and roses around me. My lifestyle come with bull shit and that's why I rarely even leave the house when I have Noelle. How can you and I coexist if we can't go anywhere and be on no real couple type of shit. I thought I was safe being in Vegas but obviously not here either! Jealous niggas live everywhere. Especially where broke niggas exist." He hit the steering wheel again with his fist.

"Hire security Chill! If your life is so dangerous then do something about it."

"I am doing something by staying away from y'all as much as I can. I don't need y'all anywhere around me!"

When he let those words leave his lips, I was so heartbroken that I didn't argue back. My eyes started to burn, and it was hard to swallow the big lump in my throat. Now I couldn't wait to get away from him. I should've never even gotten close to him anyway.

Chapter 14

Chill

Mad at myself and the situation we were just in made me go manic about finding out who robbed me. Rhino wasn't a common nickname like JJ or something like Ace. That's why I knew I could find out who he was with a little research. I got on Facebook and typed in the name Rhino and filtered the search to Nevada. It gave me about five profiles to choose from and I studied them all until I felt I hit the Jackpot.

I didn't see a face, but that stance and tattooed hands were the same as the nigga who robbed me. After a few swipes through his pictures, I spotted the gun he used sitting in his lap on some stairs. Behind the staircase was a brick that I knew was from apartments I'd been to before.

When I first came to Vegas, I needed guns and a connect hooked me up with some niggas out of these apartments. When I think about it, that's probably what put them on to me in the first place. Ain't no telling how long them niggas been watching and waiting to rob me.

"Where you burning out too Nigga?" Keys asked as I jumped up from my couch.

"I found these niggas bruh, you sliding or you hiding nigga?"

"You already know I'm slip and sliding. Just lead the way my boy."

Keys replied, pulling his pistol from his waistband and taking off the safety. We left out of the door and went downstairs to my car to take off towards the opps.

When we pulled inside the complex, we immediately saw a junkie walking down the street with a Christmas bulb necklace on. I slowed down and she walked straight up to the car.

"If y'all pretty niggas trying to buy pussy, meet me in the back by the dumpsters."

"Super fuck no." Keys scrunched up his face.

"We came here to find Rhino; we got a check for him."

"Rhino don't stay over here. His mama Paulette do."

"What apartment number does she stay in? Here's a hundred for you." I stuck a hundred-dollar bill out the window.

"No offense but you in a rolls Royce. I know you can do better than that."

I chuckled at her hustle because she knew a man with money when she saw one. I didn't like to be hustled but I admired a good hustler. I wouldn't have gotten as far as I did without getting over on people.

"Here's $600. Buy a real jacket for this wintertime."

"I sure will and imma get me some new boots." She did a little dance.

"Paulette stay in the back buildings in the townhouse units, number 5975."

"Alright bet, you have a nice night. What's your name again?"

"It's Candy." She scratched at the back of her neck.

"Alright, don't tell no one I talk to you."

"I won't. Merry Christmas from a hoe, hoe, hoe." She bounced her little ass titties before she ran off.

We drove around to the back where the complex seemed to get darker and darker. The streetlights and building lights were all knocked out.

"There ain't no lights back here. You got some flashlights in your trunk?"

"Yeah. Two of them. Just bring one though. One of us need our hand on our pistol the whole time."

When we got out of the car, we had to shine our lights just to read the numbers on the door. This 5975 is right here. Keys stepped back and kicked down the door. When we got inside, we shined the light through the apartments until we spotted a woman and kids huddled up in the corner.

When keys pointed the light towards the ceiling the cold apartment lit up with a glow. There was an older black lady with a little boy with overgrown hair and two little girls who visibly had dirt on their faces.

"Where is Rhino?"

"He don't live here anymore."

"Well you need to call him over here. He took some very important items from me that I need back."

"We don't have no phone right now."

"And why don't y'all have lights on in this mutha fucka?" Keys asked while fumbling around the dark living room.

"They're off. They been off."

"So that nigga running around robbing mutha fuckas but y'all lights off. Tragic." Keys shook his head as we stood over them.

The kids balled up on the floor wouldn't look in my direction and were all shaking but I'm not sure if it was because of fear or the temperature. I know they must be freezing in a place like this and it was inhumane, to say the least.

I hated to see this shit.

"These Rhino kids?"

"One of them is. The other two are my other grandsons. He's in jail."

"And how long y'all plan on having these kids in this condition?"

"Rhino went out tonight promising me he would have the money for tomorrow. The kids and I have been huddled together to keep warm until he comes back with the money in the morning."

Her eyes were bucked towards me, and I genuinely felt her pain. My heart went out to her because she was obviously in the middle of her neglectful son's bull shit. I don't understand niggas like him because I would never let Noelle exist in an apartment like this. Shit I hated her, and her mama stayed in an apartment to begin with.

"Y'all get up and come with me."

They all started to whine and cry

"I'm not going to hurt y'all. I just want to get y'all somewhere warm to stay tonight."

The grandmother's face lit up.

"Somewhere warm?"

"Yeah."

"Nigga what?" Keys questioned probably feeling I was being too nice.

"Man, you dragged me out in this cold to be a ol Santa Claus ass nigga tonight."

"Shut up bro. These kids innocent. They don't have shit to do with what happened to me earlier."

I turned back to them."

"So y'all coming or not?"

She sat there for a few seconds and then she finally spoke up.

"Yes, we will come if you have good intentions."

"I do so come on. We don't have all night."

Keys was shaking his head because in his mind we were supposed to smoke all of them and leave a message for Rhino. I just couldn't do it tonight and I think it's because my baby mama and my daughter have been on my mind heavy. I've never killed a kid and I never will. Especially not after having one of my own.

I took them all to a hotel nearby and paid for the room for two nights. After getting all her billing information I made note to call and pay it in the morning so they could at least go back to that apartment with heat. As far as Rhino I was still on the lookout for him and would be every day until I found him. I didn't kill kids, but I would wrap a bullet in a bow for a bum ass nigga like Rhino.

I was close to home when Keys got a text message that made him start to smile.

"Who got you that happy nigga?"

"That bitch your baby mama came here with. I'm about to go smash one more time at your crib before we go get an annulment at the twenty-four-hour Chapel."

"So you did that shit again? The Trinidad bitch last summer wasn't the only lesson you needed?"

"Man, I don't know what's wrong with me. I get drunk and then start marrying bitches. My heart may be fucked up, but it still beats for these hoes. Plus, it's too many chapels out here man. It's like asking a recovering alcoholic to go work at a Hennessy factory.

We laughed at his messed-up logic.

"Well congratulations on your 3rd marriage nigga. Me on the other hand, I'll probably never get married."

"Shid I highly doubt that. I see the way you look when you be under your baby moms. I can tell she got yo ass sprung."

I laughed off his comment because I couldn't agree or disagree. I was confused as hell and battling inside on what I needed to do with Tish. She had been giving me a feeling that I hadn't felt with a bitch not ever. But that fear in my heart I had earlier was something I think I will never get accustomed to.

I may need to go to God to figure this out.

Chapter 15

Dixon

Keys and I were fucking the pictures off the nightstand in Chill's spare bedroom. Keys was hitting my pussy from the back and playing with my clit which made me feel like I was about to go supernova. We knew this was our last go around so we had to make it count.

I climbed on top of him and started bouncing on his hard-ass dick until he started to gasp for air.

"Get up, get up."

"Unt, Unt. You told me to ride that dick so that's what I'm doing."

"I know but I'm about to nu nut." He stuttered as I clinched my walls on his dick.

"Don't worry baby, I'm on birth control." I told him and he instantly burst a big ass nut inside of me. I collapsed onto his chest and laid there panting for a few seconds until his body jerked and he reached for his chest.

"What's wrong?"

"It's my chest, get up. I need to sit up." The urgency in his voice told me he was scared, and I was too. He sat up on the side of the bed and started moaning from the pain.

"Do I need to get you some water or anything,"

"Get my pants. My medicine." He was barely able to finish the word before he curled over and sent me into a panic. Once he hit the floor I screamed to the top of my lungs before rushing for my phone. Knocks started at the door and soon a housekeeper barged into the room.

"Is everything okay?" She asked, with her eyes bulging from her head. I was naked but I didn't have time to be ashamed of my body.

"I think something is going on with his heart?"

"Oh no. Are you calling 9-1-1"

"I'm trying!"

"Yes hurry! Hurry now!" We stood over him as his eyes started to roll into the back of his head. The 911 operator got on the phone and started giving us directions on how to do CPR. The housekeeper started to perform it and I stood helpless hoping we could get him alive.

I left Keys on the floor to run into the restroom and put on my clothes. I came back out to the room to about three paramedics working around him. They loaded him up and carried him to the elevator and we were right behind them. My heart was beating out of my chest, and I felt slightly responsible for all this. Had I not fucked that man like crazy for the past few hours he probably wouldn't be on that stretcher.

Once we made it to the hospital, we stayed in the lobby for about an hour before anyone else showed up. First came Chill, then another one of their friends, and after him, Stella the baby mama.

"Chill what's going on? Is he okay?" She held a little girl on her hip as two younger boys trailed behind her.

"I don't know, I just got here. Y'all have a seat and don't panic. That won't help shit."

While breathing heavily she sat down in the chair next to Chill and he did nothing to try and comfort her.

After we sat in the waiting room for over an hour a doctor finally came into the room.

"Are you all the family of Xavier Keys?"

"Yes, that's us." Stella stood up from her seat.

"Hi, I'm Doctor Jones. I've been the cardiologist seeing Xavier since he's been here tonight."

"How is he doing? Is he awake?" Chill spoke up. From the look on the doctor's face I could tell whatever he was going to say was going to be bad.

"Mr. Keys is not awake, and we are hoping that there is a fighting chance that he will wake up. We have him in a medically induced coma because he had a heart attack and went into cardiac arrest. My colleagues and I have assessed the patient and we do feel open heart surgery is the only option to guarantee survival for this patient.

However." He took a deep breath as he looked us all eye to eye.

"We're not sure how long his heart wasn't beating and how long his lungs, kidneys, and other body parts were without oxygen."

"What does that mean?" Stella asked.

"It means his body may actually be too weak for surgery and he could die on the operating table."

Stella started to do that loud pant again and Chill looked annoyed in the face but he ignored her and asked more questions.

"So, aren't we looking at a lose lose situation? With the surgery he could die, without it he will die."

"Yes, that is correct. Now there is a rare chance that keeping him under for a few weeks can help his heart. That's in the very rare incident that he does survive long enough for that to happen.

He replied and the conversation seemed to cease for the moment. At that time, I felt tears begin to drip down my face. Why I was crying over a man I barely knew, I couldn't explain. It was just so real playing married with him earlier and it made me feel like more than a piece of meat. I felt loved, wanted, and protected, in just one day. I could only imagine feeling that every day.

"I want to let you all know that the decision is up to next of kin. We will do what you approve of in this time."

"Let's just wait it out. I mean why cut him open when he's not strong enough?" Stella spoke up.

"Yeah, but we don't know if he's strong enough to wait it out. I need to call his mama."

"She's just going to get overly worked up Chill."

"She needs to know. She will never forgive me if I didn't tell her until it was too late."

Chill and her went back and forth. The doctor patiently waited there and I was impatiently ready for them to stop arguing. I knew what my opinion was on the matter, and truth be told, right now, my opinion is the only one that matters.

"I think you should go ahead and operate on him before things turn for the worse." I raised my voice demanding their attention.

"Excuse me, who are you?" Stella adjusted her child on her hip and flared her nostrils.

"I'm Dixon."

"Well Dixon, no one asked you. I'm guessing you're the hoe he was laid up with before coming here. Damn, sticking around for one of your johns is quite honorable of you." She flamed me with her words. Just from that one interaction alone, I knew I hated this bitch. How dare she refer to me as a prostitute.

"Actually, I'm not a prostitute. I'm Keys wife." I held up my left hand.

"So, I say he gets the surgery and that's my final opinion. Where do I sign?"

Stella sat her daughter in the seat behind her and then charged towards me. Chill caught her just before she reached me and security guards in the lobby ran over to the commotion.

"His what! His who! Bitch I will kill you. Chill what the fuck is this hoe talking about?" Her voice was going in and out from the volume she was screaming. I couldn't care less right now about how she felt.

"As I was saying. Do the surgery on Xavier and I'll be right here when it's time to sign." I sat down in the chair and said a quick prayer for my medical instincts to be right. If not, then I guess I'll be a widow at this young age. A rich widow at that.

Chapter 16

Krystal

7:00 am

I didn't need to set an alarm this morning because the sun shined through the hospital windows right on time. I turned over in the pull-out chair I was sleeping in and spotted Nick still asleep in the hospital bed next to me.

I got up from my uncomfortable sleep position and folded up the cover that I slept under. After getting my jacket and my purse from the floor I crept over towards Nick whose eyes slowly opened as I stood over him.

"You leaving?"

"Yea. I have to go back to the room and pack because my flight leaves at 12:00."

"Damn, that's no news i wanted to wake up to this morning."

"Don't worry, I'll be back. Trust, I enjoyed my time here."

"In Vegas, or here as in my presence."

"A little bit of both. You were definitely the fresh air I needed on this vacation."

"And you were my savior along with the Christmas spirit I needed. Thank you again for the tree."

"You're welcome. I guess I'll see you again at some point."

"You guess? Why a guess?"

"Well, I WILL see you again. How does that sound?"

"Sounds like music to my ears. Have a safe flight home."

"Thank you, boo. Get better."

I leaned over the bed and kissed him once on the forehead before walking out of the door.

When my ride pulled up outside, I jumped inside to go to my next stop Wells Fargo. I wanted to cash my winnings and put it into my bank account before I go home. God knows if I lost this check on the flight home I would be sick to my stomach.

"Okay, stopping at Wells Fargo, correct?"

"Yes sir, thank you," I replied, putting on my seat belt. Let It Snow by Boys II Men was playing over the radio and it instantly caused my eyes to start to water. This was always one of the songs Leon and I listened to while putting up the Christmas tree. This time of the year was always our favorite in our household, now it was just about to remind me of the end of my marriage.

When we arrived at the bank I dashed inside and waited in the long line to cash my check.

"Are we depositing this or getting cash in return?"

"Deposit it. I have to get on a plane soon."

She typed numbers in the computer, ran the check through a machine, and soon gave me a receipt.

"Here you are. Merry Christmas and congratulations on your big win." She smiled, and I walked out of the bank. As I sat in the Uber, I decided to do some last-minute shopping while here and maybe some at the airport. There was no time to get stuff shipped so I was going to do pick-up orders around town for things we originally couldn't afford for the kids. I placed an order for a PlayStation 5 for junior and got my baby girl that big Barbie dream house she's been asking for. After purchasing over a thousand dollars' worth of stuff for the kids I tried to think of something I wanted for myself. Something that I truly deserved. It took me a minute, but then I finally came up with the gift for myself. I needed to gift myself a great divorce lawyer so I could leave my marriage with everything I came in plus more. I googled divorce lawyers in the Dallas area and patiently scrolled through my many options until I found a black lady who looked like she meant business. I clicked on her website and then filled out her contact form with hopes that this would be the start of an easy process. After all divorcing Leon was going to be hard but it had to be done. Especially with what I know now.

I was let out in front of the hotel and made my way through the busy lobby filled with suitcases and guests ready to go home for the holidays. My time here was fun, heartbreaking, and quite informative all in one. When I reached the room door, I took a deep breath because I didn't know how I would react to seeing Dixon again. Truth is, I was too embarrassed to even look her in the face.

"Oh, it's you." Tish turned over her shoulder as she packed her clothes into her suitcase. Just looking at her once, I noticed that she'd been crying.

"You okay?"

"Yeah, I mean it's just a lot going on. First you and Dixon are at odds then Chill and I got robbed."

"My goodness, are you okay?"

"Yeah, I'm fine. My feelings are just hurt. I'm so ready to go home now and be with my baby." She took a deep breath.

"Yeah, my time here has been interesting but I'm thankful for it. Let's just get packed and be at the airport early. The way the lobby is looking it seems like the airport will be even worse. You heard from your friend?" I snaked my neck because I was still so angry.

"Our friend said she's not leaving until tomorrow. I don't even have the strength to ask her why."

"What about her things?"

"She stopped by and got her suitcase like twenty minutes ago and then left out again. I tried telling her she needed to leave with us, but she reminded me that she travels alone all the time, so I let her be."

"Mm, she's probably with a nigga, you know how she is."

"Yeah I know, but Krystal you do know that she wouldn't do anything to hurt you. We've been real friends for so long. Please understand her position."

"I mean I can try, it's just hard right now because I don't want to look in anyone's face who my husband made moves on. Understand my position."

"And I do, and if it means anything I'm sorry things are going left with Leon."

"Thank you, I appreciate your sorrow. Let me start packing though. I can't stand here talking all day or I'm going to miss my flight."

We both shook off our conversation and started packing our clothes into our bag. Once we were done we had another three hours until our flight but we still decided to go to the airport. With my newfound small fortune, I wasn't going to have to be frugal when searching for things to snack on.

All in all, I was happy to be going home with a new revelation about relationships, friends, and my sex life which I never thought I would have before.

Chapter 17

Tish

Dallas Texas

Stopping my car in front of my sister's apartment building, I took a second to breathe before going inside. After my crazy ass trip, I got to the airport and my carry-on bag was stolen when I went to the restroom. My ID, bank cards, and everything else was gone with the thieves. Thank God Krystal had our boarding passes on her phone, or I would still be in Vegas. This had been an eventful ass few days, and I just needed my moment of peace. I closed my eyes, exhaled deeply, and then reached for the door handle. climbing out into the blistering cold.

I ran up to the door and heard Noelle's voice echoing before I knocked. When Tasha opened it, I squatted down to the floor and Noelle cheerfully ran into my arms. She had on a tan skirt, a white long-sleeve shirt, white stockings, and brown boots. I loved to play dress up on her because she was my little doll.

"So, when are you going to tell me about your time with baby daddy?"

"I promise I will in the morning. I'm sleepy as hell and want to tell the full details without leaving anything out."

"Okay, I'll be waiting.

Noelle and I lived in an apartment building near downtown called the Drake. I could only afford it because of Chill's constant money transfers. I had the apartment all my friends wanted to host parties at and gather in. The lobby was also nice, and we had a 15-foot tree coated in fake snow with a million bright lights illuminating the room. There was an infinity pool, decked-out conference rooms, and a fitness center that made Gold's Gym look like a prison yard.

"Mommy can I take a picture by the tree please."

"Of course, baby. Go ahead." I let go of her hand and she ran in front of the tree. Noelle made sure she got a picture every time we passed through the lobby. I was thinking of doing something cute with the pictures like getting them all printed onto a canvas. Then every Christmas season I would line the photos down the halls no matter how old she was. I was sure her adolescent years would be in the past because the small amount of time she's been here seems like it's flown by.

"Come on Noelle, let's go upstairs now."

I told my daughter who was busy running around the tree. When my phone started to ring, I looked and was surprised by who was calling. It was Chill, and to be honest I didn't know why. Our fling is over because I've left Vegas and he said he wanted nothing to do with me.

"Yes."

"Hello to you too mama."

"Can I help you Chill?"

"Alright, so I understand the attitude, but I just wanted to make sure you made it home okay."

"Yeah, I did. Lost my luggage but it is what it is."

"I'm sorry to hear that. Maybe someone in the airport will find it and you can release it to me so I can bring it to you."

"Bring it to me? Why would you do that?"

"Because I wanted to come down and spend Christmas with y'all. That's if you will have me." He replied, shocking the hell out of me.

"Why aren't you saying anything?" He asked because of my silence.

"Because I can't believe you want to come down."

"Well believe it. Me coming down there more often won't hurt anything. As long as you will have me." He sounded sincere at the moment.

"Of course I will have you. Noelle would really like that."

"Good, well don't tell Noelle. I want to surprise her."

"Okay, I won't."

"Alright mama, and one last thing."

"Yes?"

"I hope you will be happy to see me too. I'm sure after the last time it may be hard, but I promise I will make it up to you. I prayed on everything, and I know what I want to do."

"Okay, I will be. Just come down here and we will talk."

"Say no more. I'll see you soon mama." He replied and hung up the phone.

"Noelle, come on baby. We can make milk and cookies and watch a movie." I tried to encourage her to listen. She ran towards me with a big smile on her face and I had one too. Just that quickly Chill had turned my mood around after originally causing my heart to break.

When we got up to my apartment door, I unlocked it and entered instantly feeling at home from the scene of the peppermint fire side plug-in I got from Bath and Body Works. I sat my bags down by the door and made my way through our apartment turning the lights on. As soon as I went to take my boots off, my doorbell rang, and I raised an eyebrow.

"Who is it?"

"Flower delivery service here for Tish Gage."

I unlocked the door and opened it spotting the largest bouquet of flowers I've ever seen. There was another small bouquet of pink flowers in the other carrier's hand, so I invited them inside. Though I didn't expect flowers, I knew who they were from. Chill was working overtime on getting back in my good graces before coming here.

"These are so pretty mommy!"

"Yes, they are pretty baby. These are yours." The carriers handed us the flowers.

"Thank you both so much for delivering these." I sat the vase on the counter.

"You're welcome Ms. Gage, but one last thing."

"Yes?"

They both reached behind their backs and unexpectedly pulled out large black pistols.

"Call your baby dad and tell him you and your daughter are going to die if he doesn't wire us 50 million dollars by tomorrow." I gasped loudly and grabbed my baby.

"Y'all are coming with us, and if you scream, we're killing her first." He pointed at Noelle. My heart started to pound out of my chest, and I suddenly felt like I couldn't breathe. What the hell was happening right now?

Made in the USA
Middletown, DE
31 March 2024